AN ABUNDANCE
OF CAUTION

PAUL ANTHONY

ISBN-13: 9780974360034

Library of Congress Control Number: 2020920809

www.An-Abundance-of-Caution.com

Printed in the United States of America

Second Edition

To All People with Open Minds Who Strive for a Better World

When I first glimpsed the Jevmmunians' world—so like ours, yet so transformed by unity—I realized that humanity stands at its own threshold. Our story is not merely one of alien contact and cosmic adventure. It's a mirror held up to our deepest fears and noblest hopes. In these pages, you'll join Tobias as he learns to see beyond borders, religions, and races—beyond the limits of the physical self—and to recognize the spirit that unites us all. You'll witness a family torn apart and reassembled, a planet awakened, and a choice made: to descend into division or to rise into oneness. This is more than science fiction. It is an invitation to ask: What if we treated each other as members of one species? What if our greatest discovery is not on distant worlds, but within our own capacity for love, forgiveness, and shared purpose? If you find yourself wrestling with these questions, you have already begun the journey. Welcome to the threshold.

—Paul Anthony

Table of Contents

Chapter 1

Jevmmuns

Tobias Sinclair stood at the edge of the ramp, the forest behind him silent and still. The spacecraft loomed ahead, its surface gleaming like obsidian under the fading light. He hesitated—not because he doubted the science, but because he felt the weight of departure. This wasn't just a launch. It was a severing.

Stokes waited patiently at the top of the ramp, his expression unreadable. "It's time," he said.

Tobias stepped forward. The door sealed behind him with a quiet hiss, and the world he'd known vanished.

Inside, the ship was unexpectedly warm. Sloping windows curved along the walls, offering panoramic views of the clearing below. As the engines engaged, the forest shrank, then the hills, then the continent. Earth receded into the void—a blue marble suspended in black.

Tobias forced himself to smile back at Stokes in an attempt to avoid feeling the mixed emotions that come from having seen Earth shrink into anonymity for the first time. Like many people, he had, of course, previously seen photographs from distant space probes showing Earth as a tiny speck. Yet, those were only photographs. This was real. In one moment, he was farther away from Earth than anyone he had ever known in his life. He wondered whether this sight, and its profound implications, had touched him to feel truly free, truly lost, or truly found.

"You've been here before," Stokes said, walking beside him.

Tobias nodded. "Once. After that lecture in Manhattan."

"You were skeptical then."

"I still am."

Stokes smiled. "Good. Skepticism is the first step toward clarity."

They entered the central chamber. Tobias immediately recognized the crew—Goren, a grey extraterrestrial, hunched over a console, muttering to himself; Beatrice reviewing flight data with her usual quiet intensity. Others nodded in greetings, familiar faces from past briefings and simulations. This wasn't a crew of strangers. It was a reunion.

Then Beatrice turned.

She moved with the grace of someone who belonged everywhere and nowhere. Her eyes met Tobias's, and something in him steadied—recognition, trust, and the quiet thrill of shared purpose.

"Welcome aboard," she said. "Enjoying your first real space flight?"

"I'm awestruck," Tobias replied. "And mildly terrified."

"That's a healthy response," she said. "Let me show you to your room."

As they walked, Tobias glanced at Goren, who gave a curt wave without looking up. "Do I get the guest bedroom?"

Beatrice smiled. "Stokes warned us about your humor."

His room was modest—fold-out bed, desk, and a console embedded in the wall. Beatrice gestured to it. "This will handle your basic needs—hygiene, clothing, meals."

Tobias sat on the edge of the bed. "So this is it. I've left Earth."

Beatrice nodded. "You've left the illusion of permanence."

He looked up. "Is that what this is about? Shattering illusions?"

"In part," she said. "But mostly, it's about remembering who we are—and who we could be." Beatrice walked back to the hub of the ship while Tobias settled into his new room.

Tobias lay on the narrow bed, staring at the ceiling. The hum of the ship was constant, like a heartbeat—steady, mechanical, indifferent. He had expected exhilaration. Instead, he felt suspended, as if time itself had paused to ask him what he truly believed.

Tobias was a failed attorney who had gained some success as a writer of New Age principles. He had become fairly well-known by hosting a weekly Internet, radio, and cable program that focused on what Tobias called the "New Science." His program consisted of talks and interviews that were based on insights he'd developed after he'd suffered a head injury and seizures from a mugging incident. Yet, it was his new insights that seemed to attract the attention of the extraterrestrial community when they had acknowledged over the past two years that Tobias's emerging insights may have unintentionally placed him, and humanity, in grave danger. Tobias now wondered whether his convoluted life would ever regain even a vague semblance of normalcy. Nevertheless, it had been a long time since anything had felt "normal" in his life.

He opened the console and dimmed the lights. The stars outside sharpened into clarity, each one a silent witness to his departure. He thought of his parents, his students, the city he'd left behind. All of it now distant, abstract. He had crossed a threshold, and there was no going back.

A soft chime interrupted his thoughts. Beatrice stood at the doorway.

"Mind if I come in?"

He gestured to the chair. "Please."

She sat, folding her hands in her lap. "How are you feeling?"

"Disoriented," Tobias said. "Like I've stepped out of a story I didn't know I was part of."

Beatrice nodded. "That's normal. The mind resists scale. It clings to the familiar."

He studied her face. "Do you ever feel… detached? Like you're watching humanity from the outside?"

"All the time," she said. "But detachment isn't the goal. It's the beginning. The New Science asks us to see without flinching—to confront the arbitrary, the absurd, and still choose meaning."

Tobias leaned forward. "Is that what this mission is? A search for meaning?"

"In part," Beatrice said. "But more urgently, it's a reckoning. We've built systems that no longer serve us. We've mistaken structure for truth."

He exhaled. "And you think we're ready to face that?"

She smiled, not unkindly. "I think we're ready to try."

Beatrice settled into the chair, her posture relaxed but her eyes sharp. Tobias leaned forward, sensing the shift in tone.

"Right now, Tobias, we're headed for my home planet," she said. "We want you to witness how a civilization can navigate evolutionary turning points without collapsing into chaos."

Tobias blinked. "Wait—your home planet? I thought we were visiting the extraterrestrials."

"We are. But the planet is inhabited primarily by humans and their descendants. From Earth."

He sat up straighter. "You mean there's another world out there with Earth-born humans?"

Beatrice nodded. "Earth is my ancestral planet. My ancestors left with the Naku—what you call extraterrestrials—about forty thousand years ago."

Tobias's mind raced. "Why would they leave?"

"Because the Naku saw what was coming. Humanity had begun misusing the science they'd been taught—turning knowledge into tools of domination. They withdrew, hoping humans would evolve beyond violence and tribalism."

Tobias frowned. "You're talking about ancient civilizations—Atlantis, Lemuria?"

"Yes. The ruins still whisper their stories: Machu Picchu, Gobekli Tepe, Tiwanaku. The global society that once existed collapsed when the Naku departed."

"And they left us to figure it out?"

"To evolve," Beatrice said. "They believed that until humanity could reject warfare and embrace the sanctity of life, we weren't ready for the New Science."

Tobias stared at her, the pieces falling into place. "That's what Stokes said. That your community doesn't believe Earth is ready."

Beatrice met his gaze. "We're still watching. Still hoping."

Beatrice hesitated, then said quietly, "I'm afraid that's correct. After studying human society, we don't believe Earth is ready to use the New Science constructively."

Tobias's eyes narrowed. "When will you and the Naku ever think we're ready? Not forty thousand years ago? Not twenty? Not now? Not ever?"

Beatrice leaned forward, her voice calm but firm. "The Naku—along with the humans who live among them—learned to use an abundance of caution. Every time humans were exposed to transformative knowledge, they weaponized it. They polluted, they divided, they waged war."

Tobias stood, pacing. "So you think so little of us?"

Beatrice's expression softened. "No, Tobias. The problem is that you think so little of yourselves."

He stopped.

"When you discovered flight," she continued, "you built machines to bomb cities. When you unlocked nuclear fission, you leveled entire populations. Atlantis. Teotihuacan. Hiroshima. The pattern repeats."

Tobias sat again, quieter now.

"Even my planet," Beatrice said, "had to confront those same temptations. We nearly fell. But we chose restraint. We chose reflection."

Tobias looked at her, the weight of history pressing in. "And now you're asking me to help Earth do the same."

Beatrice nodded. "Not because we think you're ready. But because we think you might be."

As the ship descended, Tobias stood at the observation window, transfixed. Jevmmuns, named after the eight planets of the ancestral solar system, filled the glass—its curvature vast, its atmosphere swirling with blue and white streaks. It looked eerily like Earth, yet larger, with five continents arranged in unfamiliar harmony.

6

The city appeared like a mirage—rising from dry stone and sand, an oasis of cultivated trees and geometric wonder. Tobias's breath caught as they flew over pyramids and temples that mirrored Earth's ancient sites: Teotihuacán, Puma Punku, Machu Picchu, the Sphinx. But here, they were pristine, alive, and in use.

Then came the thunderclap.

The ship jolted violently, tilting at a seventy-degree angle. Tobias instinctively reached for Beatrice as they tumbled to the floor. Another strike hit near the ramp. The Naku pilots moved with silent precision, stabilizing the craft and pulling it into the stratosphere before circling back.

"Was that a weapon?" Tobias asked, shaken.

"A wave," one of the Naku said aloud. "Energy. Deliberate."

Beatrice's voice was calm but firm. "Some fear Earth's influence. They see our surveillance as a threat."

"Why?" Tobias asked. "Aren't we the same species?"

Stokes stepped in. "Yes. But many here view Earth as primitive. They fear contamination."

Tobias exhaled. "So we're barbarians now?"

"Not barbarians," Beatrice said. "Just not ready."

The ship landed without further incident on a Nazca-like airstrip, gliding into a vast spherical terminal. Silence enveloped them—a pause like the stillness after a plane taxis to the gate, or a car settles into a garage. Tobias felt it: the hush before a new mission begins.

The exit ramp jammed, dented from the earlier impact. Two terminal workers arrived to pry it open. As the crew descended, a young woman in a sleek jumpsuit greeted them.

"Welcome to Jevmmuns," she said warmly.

Tobias looked around in wonder. The terminal resembled an ultra-modern airport yet retained the intimacy of a well-designed public space. Humans and Naku moved together—alone, in pairs, in groups. Tobias estimated nine out of ten were human, but the presence of Naku was unmistakable.

He walked beside Beatrice through the corridors, which opened into tree-lined paths leading to a nearby building.

"I guess I'm not in Kansas anymore," Tobias said.

Beatrice looked puzzled. "Oh, are you originally from Kansas?"

Tobias smiled. "No, Pennsylvania. I thought you knew that."

Sunlight streaked across her face as shadows danced beneath the trees.

"I only recently joined the crew," she admitted. "I know only the basics about your life."

"So you're a newcomer yourself," Tobias said, chuckling.

Beatrice nodded. "The surveillance team asked me to help as an anthropologist. They thought you might need help adjusting to our society."

"Adjusting to what, exactly?"

"We'll explain more at the senior staff meeting," she said, then paused. "But what does any of this have to do with Kansas?"

"It's a line from a movie—*The Wizard of Oz*," Tobias said, pleased to know something she didn't.

Beatrice smiled, finally.

As they walked through the tree-lined path, Tobias glanced at the passing humans and Naku, marveling at the calm, purposeful energy of the city. The pyramidal buildings shimmered in the pale sunlight, surrounded by lush vegetation and interlaced with gentle footpaths.

"I've studied many sentient species," Beatrice said, "but Earth has always fascinated me."

"Fascinated?" Tobias asked.

"Yes. The way your planet evolved in response to shared challenges—so differently from ours."

Tobias cracked a smile. "Trying to get in touch with your roots, eh?"

Beatrice bristled slightly, but her voice remained composed. "Studying Earth has been both rewarding and intriguing. Personally and professionally."

"What do you find intriguing?" Tobias asked.

"The way you govern yourselves," she said. "Earth divides itself into nations—uncoordinated, often unjust. On Jevmmuns, we prioritize the species over the structure."

Tobias nodded slowly. "So you have a global government?"

"A sovereign planet," she corrected. "Regional differences exist, but every region is part of the same whole."

They paused beneath a sycamore-like tree. Beatrice looked directly at him. "Is it true that people on Earth kill each other over how to govern?"

Tobias looked down at the budding flowers. "Yes. Over borders, beliefs, skin color, language, even water and stones."

Beatrice's voice softened. "I can see why you left."

Tobias smiled faintly. "Still intrigued?"

"I am," she said. "I've even gone undercover on Earth. Briefly."

Tobias turned, surprised. "Have we met before?"

Beatrice hesitated. "We may have crossed paths."

They arrived at a sandstone building. The entrance slid open automatically.

"This is where we'll meet the others," she said.

Inside, the corridor led to a conference room. Beatrice paused. "I've attended your lectures. Online and in person. I stayed quiet in the audience."

Tobias smiled. "You've been keeping an eye on me."

They shared a glance, then entered the room.

Fifteen humans and five Naku were already seated around a sleek oblong table. Stokes and Goren stood near the entrance, chatting with colleagues. Beatrice greeted a few warmly; they nodded at Tobias with quiet respect.

A chime rang from the ceiling.

An older man with a full head of curly white hair stood. "Everyone, please be seated."

Beatrice leaned in. "You're the guest of honor, Tobias. We'll sit together."

They took seats near the front. The room fell silent.

The man looked directly at Tobias. "This is one of those moments when words fail. As Senior Advisor of our research division, it is an honor to witness the transformation of our mother planet's people into creatures of reason."

He smiled. "Forgive us, Tobias. We don't mean to overwhelm you with our dedication to Earth."

Tobias looked from Beatrice to the man with white curls, then swept his gaze across the room. He nodded slowly, unsure of what to say.

"I'm Murray," the man said. "Head of the Earth Surveillance Program. Everyone here is part of the Council. We made the decision to reveal ourselves to you—and through you, to Earth."

Tobias remained silent.

"We believe Earth is approaching a crossroads," Murray continued. "Your teachings—the New Science—represent a leap forward. But they also placed you in grave danger. Without our intervention, your work might have ended before it began."

"I know," Tobias said quietly. "I almost didn't make it here."

Murray frowned. "What do you mean?"

Beatrice spoke up. "There was an attack on our spacecraft during landing. A sonic weapon. Likely from extremists."

Murray's expression darkened. "I'm sorry, Tobias. I hope no one was harmed."

"No," Beatrice said. "But the threat is real. We hope it won't deter Tobias from continuing with us."

Murray turned to Tobias. "If you choose to join us, you can help expand the realm of human existence."

Tobias blinked. "Join you? I just got here. I don't know who you are, or what Jevmmuns really is. Isn't that a bit much?"

A few Council members smiled gently.

"We've watched Earth for millennia," Murray said. "From Egypt to Rome, Zimbabwe to the Aztecs. We've seen your wars, your genocides, your enslavement. And now, we see your civilization teetering again—caught between technological advancement and human nature."

Tobias looked around the table. "Why me?"

"Your writings," Murray said. "Your lectures. Your 'Day of Forgiveness' campaign."

Tobias chuckled nervously. "So my books led me to a flying saucer? I always knew my work would take me far, but this is ridiculous."

Laughter rippled through the room. Tobias relaxed slightly.

"I tried to help people see themselves as one species," he said. "But the campaign failed. I was called a fraud."

Beatrice touched his shoulder. "The idea was right. The execution was flawed. And the threats against you—especially from the Children of the Light— made it dangerous."

Stokes nodded. "I told Tobias about them before we left Earth."

Goren, seated across the room, sent a telepathic message directly to Tobias: *It goes deeper than that.*

Tobias flinched. The voice in his mind felt like an intrusion.

12

"You're sensitive to telepathy," Goren said aloud. "That's why you were chosen."

"Chosen for what?" Tobias asked.

Goren stood and walked toward him. "We've been sending you messages since 1995. You thought they were your own ideas—but they were ours."

Tobias stared at him. "My thoughts weren't mine?"

"Not entirely," Goren said. "*We* suggested you leave law. *We* nudged you to write your first book. *We* guided your shift toward helping humanity."

Tobias's voice rose. "You manipulated my life! My career, my family—without asking!"

"We believed it was for the greater good," Murray said. "Cliché, yes. But true."

Tobias shook his head. "You've been watching too much of our sci-fi."

Goren continued, "You were the most receptive. You believed the messages came from your future self, and thus, trusted those thoughts. That made you open to our influence."

Stokes added gently, "After your head injury, your sensitivity increased. You began to read our minds as we read yours. Your seizures amplified the connection."

Tobias sat back, stunned. "So the New Science wasn't mine?"

"It was ours," Murray said. "But you gave it form. You gave it voice."

Beatrice leaned in. "We want you to use your program to introduce Earth to its cousins—to us."

13

Tobias frowned. "People barely accepted the New Science. How can I convince them of extraterrestrials?"

"One of our crew will appear on your show," Murray said.

Tobias exhaled. "You want me to blow your cover?"

"Yes," Murray replied. "Gently. Thoughtfully."

Goren added, "Earth is ripe for contact—not because it's ready, but because it's on the brink."

Beatrice touched Tobias's arm. "Knowledge is the path. Understanding breeds love. Fear comes from the unknown."

Tobias looked at her. "You're asking me to help humanity avoid self-destruction. That's a lot."

Beatrice nodded. "It is. But you're not alone."

Murray struck a small chime. "Let's pause here. Tobias needs time to reflect."

The meeting was adjourned. Warm greetings were exchanged. Tobias stood, still absorbing the weight of what he'd heard.

As the meeting adjourned, Tobias lingered near the doorway, still absorbing the weight of what he'd heard. The room had emptied quickly, but the questions remained.

Stokes approached, his expression thoughtful. "You're the first human visitor who wasn't abducted or born into this society. The extremists don't know what to make of you. They act from fear."

"They don't like visitors?" Tobias asked. "Immigrants?"

14

"They don't like change," Stokes replied. "Some believe your presence marks a new beginning. Others think it's the beginning of the end."

Beatrice joined them. "Most Jevmmunians are indifferent. But those who care fall into two camps—those who want to reconnect with Earth, and those who fear contamination."

"They forget we can control tourism and immigration," she added. "Their fears are primal."

"Primal?" Tobias asked.

Beatrice nodded. "It's the ancestral tension—the rebellion against one's origins. Jevmmunians reject Earthlings like teenagers reject their parents. They call Earthlings 'primitive,' the way kids call their parents 'square.'"

Tobias smirked. "Growing pains, huh? Do they think they're too grown-up to deal with a visiting cousin like me?"

Stokes's tone turned serious. "After the attack on our ship, it's best you stay with me. Normally, you'd explore on your own. But this wasn't just a protest—it was a warning."

"Some protest," Tobias muttered.

"We don't use bodyguards here," Stokes said. "But there may be others who protest in… unconventional ways."

Tobias sighed. "This whole trip has been unconventional."

He looked at Stokes and smiled. "You visited my apartment in Brooklyn before our first trip. I guess one good turn deserves another. I'll be honored to return the favor as your houseguest."

They exchanged a quiet grin—two men caught between worlds, trying to make sense of what came next

Chapter 2

The Walk to the Museum

The morning sun cast a pale gold across the city as Tobias stepped out of Stokes's apartment. The air was dry but fragrant, tinged with minerals and something floral he couldn't name. He had slept, but not deeply. The Council meeting still echoed in his mind—telepathic manipulation, ancestral abandonment, and the weight of a task he hadn't asked for.

Beatrice was waiting outside, dressed in a simple slate-gray jumpsuit. She smiled as he approached.

"Good morning, Tobias. I thought we'd take a walk."

"A walk?" he asked, still groggy.

"There's something I want to show you."

They moved through the city's quiet streets, past pyramidal buildings and cultivated gardens. Tobias noticed how seamlessly nature and architecture blended—no fences, no traffic, no noise. Just movement and intention.

"Where are we going?" he asked.

"You'll see."

The morning air was crisp and dry, tinged with the scent of nectar and flowering trees. Tobias walked beside Beatrice along a gently curving path lined with polished stone and low vegetation. The city was quiet, but alive—its pyramidal buildings rising like ancient sentinels, surrounded by cultivated gardens and soft footpaths.

Occasional passersby nodded or offered the Jevmmunian equivalent of "Good morning." One older man, with a regal bearing and a voice like velvet, held Tobias's gaze a moment longer than expected.

Tobias smiled and nodded, careful not to speak until the man had passed. "Are the older people on Jevmmuns always this friendly?" he asked.

Beatrice glanced at him. "When they see a man like you, they see something in themselves. Many older Jevmmunians still cling to outdated ways of identifying people by ethnicity."

"My ethnicity?" Tobias asked, surprised. "African American?"

"You appear to be a blend—African, European, and more. That blend is what they recognize."

Tobias nodded. "So… are there many older Black Jevmmunians?"

Beatrice paused. "Black Jevmmunians? Tobias, Jevmmuns isn't like Earth. They don't identify with you because you're Black. They identify with you because you're White."

Tobias stopped walking. "What are you talking about?"

"Before our enlightenment, Jevmmunian society mirrored Earth's developmental stages—agriculture, industrialization, conquest. But due to our planetary tilt and land distribution, our dominant explorers resembled Africans in appearance. They became the privileged class. The oppressed resembled Europeans."

Tobias stared at his brown hands. "So I'm white here?"

"Historically, yes. But today, you're just considered human."

They sat on a nearby bench as Tobias absorbed the inversion. "So the conquerors here were Black, and the oppressed were White?"

Beatrice nodded. "The behavior was the same—exploration, invasion, enslavement. Only the roles were reversed."

Tobias shook his head. "Human behavior is human behavior."

He smiled faintly. "There was a film years ago—*White Man's Burden*. Harry Belafonte played the privileged elite. John Travolta was the oppressed minority."

Beatrice smiled. "Unlike *The Wizard of Oz*, I've seen that one."

"There's a difference, though," Beatrice added. "On Jevmmuns, Belafonte's character would've been considered White—and oppressed. Anyone with mixed ancestry would've been lumped with the lower class."

Tobias chuckled. "So I'm Black on Earth and White on Jevmmuns. I would've been sunk in both worlds."

Beatrice laughed softly. "Yes. But here, you're just human."

Tobias nodded, his smile fading. The museum loomed ahead, its sandstone walls glowing in the morning light. Whatever awaited him inside, he knew it would challenge everything he thought he understood—about history, identity, and himself.

The museum's central gallery was quiet, its vaulted ceiling casting soft shadows over the polished stone floor. Tobias and Beatrice moved slowly past holographic displays of ancient Earth civilizations—Machu Picchu, Teotihuacán, the Sphinx—each rendered in perfect detail. The translation earpiece in Tobias's ear hummed gently, allowing him to understand the Jevmmunian dialects spoken in the exhibits.

A console valet hovered nearby, silently projecting helpful prompts and offering refreshments. Tobias ignored it, his attention drawn to a large amphitheater-style display at the center of the room. They continued to walk around the museum's nearly empty main room, which had transparent cases and displays of photographs, brief videos, statues of important inventors, and historical representations of milestones in Jevmmunian history, including the first landing on each of their two moons.

Beatrice casually informed Tobias about the meaning of each display in relation to Jevmmunian progress. She said, "Despite our technological advancements, true knowledge and enlightenment were slow in coming." They stopped in front of a large doorway at the far end of the main gallery. Beatrice stood at the broad opening and nodded toward the adjacent room, which appeared to be a darker, shadowy space with subdued lighting and subtle green and blue illumination that glowed from beneath the prism like glass floor.

"This room, Tobias, is the main reason that I brought you here." Above the wide, arched opening leading into the room was a name etched in marble in Jevmmunian letters that resembled hieroglyphics.

Tobias looked up at the lettering and asked Beatrice, "What does it say?"

"It is the name of one of our greatest leaders, the person who brought us to true enlightenment, the person who changed Jevmmunian society by introducing us to a new way of thinking about ourselves and our world: Greta Stokes."

"Greta *Stokes?*"

"Yes, Tobias," replied Beatrice. "She is the sister of Thaddeus Stokes."

"His sister is a historical figure?"

"Yes," she said. "You must remember that it is common for people on Jevmmuns to live for hundreds of years due to Naku technology." She smiled, "Here, our Founding Mother is still alive."

In a hologram near the entrance, Greta Stokes stood at a podium, surrounded by a stadium of seated listeners. The video flickered to life, and her voice rang out—clear, commanding, timeless.

"If our world is based on wars, guns, bombs, and violence from political, racial, ethnic, socioeconomic, and religious differences, then we have fallen far short of the high potential that a species of our intelligence and ingenuity should possess. This behavior is beneath our species. We are not animals; we are human."

Tobias felt the words settle into him like a weight he hadn't known he was carrying.

"How long ago was this?" he asked.

"About 250 years," Beatrice replied. "Before the Naku returned. Greta's speeches helped shift our society—and convinced the Naku we were ready."

The video continued:

"No one alive today was an invader, conqueror, or enslaver. No one alive today was conquered or enslaved. We who live in modern times recognize that we were all born into the present set of circumstances. We could not keep alive the wrongful actions of long-dead unenlightened people."

The crowd in the video erupted in applause. Tobias glanced at Beatrice.

"She changed everything," he said.

"She still is," Beatrice replied. "Stokes will likely introduce you to her before we return to Earth."

Another clip played—Greta, younger, speaking to a more skeptical audience.

"Warfare is behavior that should be beneath our intelligent species. Humans are created by God. Governments are created by humans. Which is more important: the human or the government?"

Tobias whispered, "This is what I tried to say with the Day of Forgiveness."

Beatrice nodded. "And that's why we chose you."

They stood in silence, watching the final clip fade. Then Beatrice turned to Tobias and touched his arm.

"The society you see today on Jevmmuns is a direct result of Greta's enlightenment. Don't you see, Tobias? You could be the next Greta Stokes on your home planet."

Tobias didn't respond. His gaze had shifted to the far end of the gallery, where a hybrid man and a human woman were strolling casually. The man's face was human but subtly elongated—his skull shaped like a Naku's. The woman had platinum-blonde hair and striking blue eyes. Tobias thought she looked eerily like Taylor Swift.

"Weren't those two walking behind us earlier?" he asked quietly.

Beatrice glanced over. "Yes. Apparently, they were headed in the same direction."

"They're not looking at the exhibits," Tobias said. "They're looking at *us*."

Beatrice raised an eyebrow. "Do I detect a little Earthlike paranoia?"

Before Tobias could reply, the couple entered the Greta Stokes room and walked directly toward them.

"Hello," the man said in Jevmmunian.

Beatrice responded politely. Tobias nodded, remembering not to speak.

21

The strangers wandered the room, pausing at displays but never lingering. Tobias leaned toward Beatrice. "They're watching us."

Beatrice's expression hardened. "I think we should leave."

As they turned toward the exit, the woman called out. "Excuse me. We're historical researchers. May we ask a few questions about your thoughts on Greta Stokes?"

Beatrice replied firmly, "I'm sorry, but we were just leaving."

"It would only take a few minutes," the woman said.

"Maybe next time," Beatrice said.

The man stepped forward, his tone suddenly sharp—both verbal and telepathic. "Who do you think you're fooling? We know who you are."

Tobias froze. The man's dark eyes locked onto him.

"Have you forgotten that many of us have well-developed telepathic abilities?" he said. "Did you really believe this man from Earth would simply blend in?"

Beatrice held her ground. "Who are you?"

"My name is Wyman," he said, gesturing to the woman. "And this is Jem. We know about your plan to introduce Earth and Jevmmuns. We're devoted to the same cause."

Beatrice's voice was steady. "Then why follow us?"

Jem smiled. "Perhaps we can walk together. We may have information that's useful to you."

Tobias glanced at Beatrice. She remained poised, her calm demeanor now clearly a shield.

"We appreciate your concern," Beatrice said. "But if you have something important to share, you can say it here."

Wyman softened. "We realized you were taking a risk by bringing Tobias Sinclair here. We assumed you believed he could blend in—because most Jevmmunians avoid telepathic contact with strangers."

Tobias finally spoke. "Who are *we*?"

Jem answered. "We're part of a group called COL. We travel to Earth regularly."

Beatrice feigned ignorance. "We haven't heard of you."

"We're a secret organization," Jem said. "Our goal is the same as yours—first contact."

"Why in secret?" Tobias asked.

Wyman hesitated. "Because our methods aren't always considered above board. Some believe COL interferes too much with Earth's development."

Tobias frowned. "Did you?"

Jem nodded. "You wouldn't be here if it weren't for COL. We tracked you since your head injury. We helped organize your followers."

"You mean the Children of the Light?" Tobias asked.

"Yes, our Earth-based people," Wyman said. "We couldn't tell them about Jevmmuns or the Naku. It would've been too much. But we tried to guide them. And you."

Tobias looked at Beatrice. "Did COL interfere too much?"

Beatrice didn't answer. Her eyes remained fixed on Wyman.

Jem stepped closer. "We thought we were helping. But the knowledge we shared spiraled out of control."

Tobias exhaled. "Then maybe it's time we all stop hiding."

The museum's sandstone walls seemed to close in as Wyman and Jem stood before Tobias and Beatrice, their expressions unreadable. The air had shifted— no longer cordial, no longer curious. It was charged.

"We fear your team, The Council, has misjudged the timing," Wyman said. "Earth isn't ready. And neither is Jevmmuns."

Beatrice stepped forward. "We appreciate your concern. But this isn't your decision."

Jem's voice was calm, almost melodic. "We're not here to argue. We're here to redirect."

Tobias glanced toward the exit. "Redirect?"

That's when the third figure appeared—a tall Naku man with pale green skin and deep-set eyes. He moved silently, blocking the hallway that led back to the city.

Beatrice's voice dropped. "We need to leave. Now."

Tobias nodded. The console valet, still hovering nearby, chimed softly as Beatrice tapped a command into her wrist device. The valet projected a directional map and activated a privacy shield around them—an iridescent shimmer that distorted their outlines.

"Follow me," Beatrice whispered.

24

They darted through a side corridor, past holographic displays and archival kiosks. Tobias's heart pounded. He could hear footsteps behind them—measured, deliberate.

"Why are they chasing us?" he asked.

"Because they think they're protecting Earth," Beatrice said. "But they're protecting a version of Earth that no longer exists."

They burst through a service exit and into the open air. The city was quiet, the sun was low on the horizon. Beatrice scanned the skyline, then pointed toward a narrow footpath winding through a grove of flowering trees.

"This way."

They ran. Tobias stumbled once, catching himself on a low stone wall. The translation earpiece buzzed with ambient alerts—proximity warnings, encrypted signals. He ignored them.

Behind them, Wyman's voice rang out—telepathic and verbal. *You're making a mistake, Tobias. You don't know what you're walking into.*

Tobias didn't respond. He focused on Beatrice's silhouette ahead of him, her movements fluid and purposeful.

They reached a transport hub—a small platform with a single pod waiting. Beatrice keyed in a code. The door slid open.

"Get in," she said.

Tobias hesitated. "Where are we going?"

"To Stokes's apartment. He'll know what to do."

Paul Anthony

They stepped inside. The pod sealed, and with a soft hum, it lifted into the air—gliding above the city, away from the museum, away from COL.

Tobias sat back, breathless. "I didn't expect to be chased by aliens in a museum today."

Beatrice smiled faintly. "Welcome to Jevmmuns."

The transport pod hummed quietly as it glided above the city, its curved walls casting soft reflections of the Jevmmunian skyline. Tobias sat across from Beatrice, his breath still uneven from the chase. The adrenaline had faded, but the questions hadn't.

Beatrice broke the silence. "You handled that well."

Tobias shook his head. "I didn't handle anything. I just ran."

"You ran with purpose," she said. "That matters."

He looked out the window, watching the pyramids shrink beneath them. "I thought I was coming here to teach. To share ideas. Not to be hunted."

Beatrice leaned forward. "You are here to teach. But teaching truth always comes with resistance."

Tobias turned to her. "Why me? Why not someone stronger, more prepared?"

Beatrice hesitated. "Because you're not afraid to feel. That's what makes you dangerous to the old systems—and valuable to the new ones."

He studied her face. "You always seem so composed. Like nothing rattles you."

She smiled faintly. "It's a shield. I've needed it."

Tobias nodded. "I noticed. Back in the museum, when Wyman stepped forward… you didn't flinch."

"I've been trained to expect confrontation," she said. "But I wasn't trained to care."

Tobias looked down. "And now?"

Beatrice's voice softened. "Now I care."

The pod slowed as it approached Stokes's apartment complex—a sleek, low-rise structure nestled between flowering trees and stone walkways. Tobias exhaled.

"I don't know what's waiting for me in there," he said. "But I'm glad you're here."

Beatrice touched his hand briefly. "You're not alone, Tobias. Not anymore."

The transport pod touched down with a gentle thud on a stone platform nestled between flowering trees and low, pyramidal buildings. As the doors slid open, Tobias gazed out into the fading light of Jevmmuns, feeling both more grounded and more uncertain than ever. Tobias stepped out beside Beatrice, still shaken from the chase, but steadied by her presence.

Stokes's apartment was modest—clean lines, natural materials, and a quiet elegance that reflected Jevmmunian values. No guards. No fanfare. Just a simple door and a soft chime that rang as they entered.

The apartment was quiet, bathed in the soft glow of Jevmmunian twilight. Tobias and Beatrice stepped inside, still catching their breath from the chase. The console valet adjusted the lighting automatically, casting a warm amber hue across the room.

Stokes was already there, preparing drinks at a small counter. He turned and smiled. "You made it. I was starting to worry."

"We had company," Beatrice said.

Stokes nodded knowingly. "Wyman and Jem?"

Tobias raised an eyebrow. "You knew?"

"They've been circling our work for years," Stokes replied. "But tonight, you're safe."

He gestured toward the seating area, where a woman stood near the window, her silhouette framed by the fading light.

"Greta," he said gently, "I'd like you to meet Tobias Sinclair."

She turned, her expression warm and unassuming. Tobias recognized her instantly from the museum holograms, but in person, she was strikingly human—no aura of celebrity, no air of superiority. Just presence.

"I've heard much about you," she said, extending her hand.

Tobias took it, surprised by the strength in her grip. "I've heard even more about you."

Greta smiled. "Then we're even."

Beatrice leaned in. "Greta walks freely among our people. On Jevmmuns, we don't idolize our leaders. We honor their ideas, not their image."

Greta nodded. "Fame is a mirror. It reflects what people project. I prefer to walk without reflections."

Stokes returned with four glasses—clear, stemless vessels filled with a pale blue liquid that shimmered faintly.

"A local blend," he said. "Non-alcoholic, but celebratory."

They gathered around a low table. Stokes raised his glass.

"To Tobias," he said. "May your journey be guided by truth, and may your voice help Earth remember what it means to be human."

Greta added, "And may your courage inspire others to rise above what divides them."

Beatrice smiled. "To possibility."

Tobias hesitated, then raised his glass. "To all of you—for not giving up on us."

They clinked glasses. The moment was quiet but charged with meaning.

Greta sat beside Tobias. "You've been asked to do something extraordinary. But you're not alone. We've all walked through fire to get here."

Tobias looked at her. "And you still believe we're worth saving?"

Greta's eyes softened. "I believe we're worth understanding. And that's the first step."

The glasses were still warm in their hands, the pale blue liquid shimmering faintly as the four of them sat together in Stokes's apartment. Tobias felt the tension of the day slowly dissolved into quiet curiosity.

Thaddeus leaned back and gestured toward his sister. "Greta doesn't need an introduction, but I'll give one anyway. She's not just my sister—she's the reason Jevmmuns didn't collapse under its own weight centuries ago."

Greta smiled gently. "That's generous, Thaddeus. But I was just one voice among many. I happened to speak at the right time."

Tobias turned to her. "Your speeches… they were powerful. I saw them in the museum. You said things I've tried to say for years—but you said them better."

Greta nodded. "I didn't say anything new. I said what people already knew but were afraid to admit. That violence is beneath us. That division is a distraction. That forgiveness is the only way forward."

She paused, then continued. "We had to face the truth: we were all born into a story already in progress. The only choice we had was whether to continue it—or rewrite it."

Tobias leaned forward. "And you rewrote it."

Greta's eyes softened. "We all did. Together. But it started with a shift in thinking. We stopped asking who was to blame and started asking who was willing to heal."

Beatrice added, "That's why your 'Day of Forgiveness' resonated with us. It wasn't perfect, but it was a beginning."

Greta turned to Tobias. "You're not here to be perfect. You're here to be honest. To help Earth remember that it's not too late."

Tobias looked down at his glass. "I'm not sure *I'm* ready."

Greta smiled. "None of us were. But readiness isn't a prerequisite for truth. It's a consequence."

Thaddeus raised his glass again. "To truth, then. And to the courage it demands."

They toasted once more, the sound of glass meeting glass echoing softly in the quiet room.

Outside, the city of Jevmmuns pulsed with quiet life. Inside, a new chapter was beginning.

Later, the evening light had dimmed to a soft violet as Tobias sat quietly in Stokes's apartment, still absorbing Greta's words. The toast, the warmth, the philosophical clarity—it had all felt like a turning point. But the moment was short-lived.

Stokes entered from the adjoining room, his expression unusually tense.

"Tobias," he said gently, "I need to speak with you privately."

Beatrice and Greta exchanged glances and quietly stepped out, leaving the two men alone.

Stokes sat across from Tobias, his voice low. "The Council met again after our gathering. They've made a decision."

Tobias leaned forward. "What kind of decision?"

"Due to COL's awareness of your presence here—and their attempt to intercept you—the Council believes it's too risky to keep you on Jevmmuns any longer."

Tobias blinked. "You're sending me back?"

Stokes nodded. "Soon. Before COL has a chance to sabotage the plan for first contact."

Tobias stood, pacing. "But I haven't even begun to prepare. I thought I'd have time to understand more—to plan the broadcast."

"We'll help you," Stokes said. "But the window is closing. COL's reach is growing. They've already tried to block your return."

Tobias stopped pacing. "So this is it? I go back to Earth and tell everyone that aliens exist? That I've been living among them?"

"Not everyone," Stokes said. "Just enough to start the shift. The Council believes your voice can open the door—gently, strategically."

Tobias exhaled. "And if I fail?"

Stokes looked him in the eye. "Then we try again. But we believe in you, Tobias. We've seen what your words can do."

Tobias sat down slowly. "I'm not sure I believe in myself."

Stokes smiled. "That's why you're perfect for this."

That night before his departure, Tobias sat quietly on the balcony of Stokes's apartment, overlooking the softly lit cityscape of Jevmmuns. The pyramids glowed faintly in the distance, their edges softened by the pale blue atmosphere. He felt the weight of everything—what he'd learned, what he'd lost, and what he was being asked to do.

Greta joined him, carrying two cups of a warm herbal blend. She handed one to Tobias and sat beside him.

"You look like a man staring into the abyss," she said gently.

Tobias smiled faintly. "I'm trying to decide if I'm falling into it—or climbing out."

Greta sipped her drink. "Both, probably. That's how transformation works."

They sat in silence for a moment, the breeze brushing past them like a whisper.

"I don't know if I'm ready," Tobias said. "I don't know if I'm the right person."

Greta turned to him. "You're not the right person. You're the present person. That's more important."

Tobias looked at her. "You changed your world. You gave people a new way to think. I'm not sure I can do that."

Greta smiled. "I didn't change the world. I reminded it of what it already knew. You'll do the same."

He nodded slowly. "They're rushing me back. COL knows I'm here. The Council doesn't want to risk sabotage."

Greta's expression remained calm. "Then you go back with urgency. But not with fear."

Tobias stared into his cup. "What if they don't listen?"

Greta leaned in. "Some won't. But some will. And that's enough to begin."

She placed her hand over his. "You're not going back to convince the world. You're going back to awaken it."

Tobias felt something shift inside him—a quiet resolve, like a flame catching in the dark.

Greta stood. "Get some rest. Tomorrow, you begin again."

As she walked back inside, Tobias remained on the balcony, watching the stars. He didn't feel ready. But he felt willing. And that, he realized, was the beginning of everything.

Chapter 3

The Decision

The morning light filtered softly through the windows of Stokes's apartment. Tobias sat at the edge of the low couch, still absorbing the weight of his final conversation with Greta. Her words echoed in his mind: *You're not going back to convince the world. You're going back to awaken it.*

Stokes entered the room, his expression unusually serious.

"Tobias," he said, "The Council has made a final decision. You're leaving today."

Tobias stood. "Today?"

Stokes nodded. "COL's reach is growing. We've intercepted signals suggesting they may attempt to block your return. The Council believes it's too risky to wait."

Tobias exhaled. "So I go back now. Before I'm ready."

"You're more ready than you think," Stokes said. "You've seen our society. You've met Greta. You've felt the tension between what is and what could be."

Tobias paced. "And I'm supposed to go back and tell people about Jevmmuns? That everyone must evolve for the better?"

"Not everyone," Stokes said. "Just enough to start the shift. Your broadcast will be the first step."

Tobias stopped. "And if it fails?"

Stokes smiled faintly. "Then we try again. The alternative is unthinkable."

The gentle, occasional foot traffic in front of the Council building belied the crucial decisions that were being made inside. Tobias stood inside near the entrance, waiting for Stokes to emerge from a meeting, still absorbing the whirlwind of revelations from the night before. He had been chosen. He had been guided. And now, he was being sent back.

Stokes approached, his expression calm but resolute.

"Tobias," he said, "The Council has finalized its decision. You'll be returning to Earth today."

Tobias nodded slowly. "I figured as much."

"But you won't be going alone," Stokes added. "Beatrice, Goren, and I will accompany you. Along with two Naku navigators."

Tobias blinked. "You're all coming?"

Stokes smiled. "We're not sending you into the storm without a crew."

Beatrice stepped forward, along with the Naku, Goren. "We'll help you prepare the broadcast. Goren will appear on the program. And we'll stay close— until it's no longer safe."

Tobias glanced at Goren, who nodded silently, his grayish-green skin, large, elongated head and huge black eyes symbolizing an otherworldly intelligence. His presence was grounding, if still unsettling.

"COL knows you're here," Stokes continued. "They've already tried to stop us once. The Council believes they'll try again. That's why we're accelerating the timeline."

Tobias exhaled. "So I go back to Earth, still anonymous, and try to show people that they are not alone and need to navigate through a crucial stage of our evolution."

"Think of it as an awareness campaign," Beatrice said. "Introduce the concepts. Familiarity breeds understanding."

Tobias looked out the window, watching the Jevmmunian city stir to life. "And what happens after the broadcast?"

Stokes hesitated. "We don't know. But we'll be with you. Until we can't be."

Goren's voice echoed telepathically in Tobias's mind: *The truth is always worth the risk.*

Tobias turned to face them. "Then let's go."

Tobias boarded the spacecraft in silence, walking behind Goren but ahead of Stokes and Beatrice. His steps were heavy, his thoughts darker than he cared to admit. The others could sense it—his emotional turmoil rippling through the cabin like static. No words were spoken, but the tension was palpable.

Beatrice approached him gently and touched his arm. "Do you want to talk about it?"

Tobias hesitated, then nodded. "Yes."

They walked together down the corridor toward Tobias's quarters. As they passed the observation window, Tobias glanced back at Jevmmuns—blue, white, and dusted with clouds—shrinking into the void.

"I feel like an old pro on this ship," he said, trying to mask his unease.

"You're getting there," Beatrice replied with a faint smile.

Inside his quarters, Tobias sat on the bed while Beatrice took the chair. The room was spotless, as if someone had tidied it while they were away.

"I guess I wear my heart on my sleeve around here," Tobias said.

Beatrice nodded. "We don't eavesdrop on thoughts. That would be invasive. But we can sense emotions—especially fear, anger, and sadness."

Tobias's voice rose. "Anger? Can you blame me? You manipulated my mind. You rewrote my life. I left behind my son, my family, my friends—and for what?"

Beatrice's voice was soft. "We need you, Tobias. The world needs you."

Tobias stood, pacing. "Which world? Yours? Earth? You used me to serve your agenda. You didn't ask. You just intervened."

"It's not fair to say we don't care," Beatrice said. "Earth is on the brink. We're trying to help prevent another collapse. Isn't that worth something?"

Tobias turned sharply. "A sacrifice only counts if it's voluntary. Otherwise, it's just slaughter."

Beatrice looked at him, her eyes steady. "Do you really believe we're sending you to slaughter? We're asking you to help prevent one."

Tobias paused, staring through the open door into the corridor. His voice dropped. "You want me to teach forgiveness. Can you forgive me for not being ready?"

Beatrice leaned in. "Can you forgive us for believing in you?"

Tobias didn't answer. But something in him softened.

Beatrice stood and stepped toward the doorway. "I think we've had a good talk. I no longer sense any anger from you."

Tobias rose slowly. "What do you sense instead?"

She paused in the corridor, her silhouette framed by the soft hallway light. "Bewilderment," she said gently, and the door slid shut behind her.

Tobias sat back down on the bed, removed his shoes, and stretched out. Her words lingered. So did Greta's, from the night before. They drifted beneath the surface of his mind, like sediment stirred by a passing current.

His usual response to discomfort was to run. From Philadelphia to New York. From New York to Jevmmuns. But now, he wasn't sure where there was left to run.

Oddly, Jevmmuns had brought him closer to Earth. Closer to himself.

He stared at the ceiling, wondering what kind of life he'd return to. Wondering if the people he loved would still recognize him. Wondering if he still recognized himself.

Eventually, sleep came—not peaceful, but necessary. And somewhere in the quiet hum of the spacecraft, Tobias began to prepare for the world he was about to reenter.

Tobias sat alone at the desk in his quarters aboard the spacecraft, the Earth visible through the observation window behind him. He picked up his cell phone—miraculously charged by the Jevmmunian console—and dialed David.

"Hello? Pop, is that you?"

Tobias smiled faintly. "Damn that caller ID. I could never surprise you."

David's voice was tense. "I tried to call you. Your phone always went straight to voicemail."

"I was far away," Tobias said gently. "How's Grandma? Aunt Janice?"

"They're hanging in. But Pop—where were you? You said you'd be gone for a few weeks. It's been months."

Tobias winced. "I know. It must've felt like forever."

"You left without warning. I had to explain everything to them. We didn't know what to think."

"I'm sorry, David. I should've told them myself. I had to leave quickly. There wasn't time."

David's voice softened, but the hurt lingered. "Are you back in New York?"

"Not quite. But I'm back. And I'll see you soon."

"What's going on, Pop? What's the big secret?"

Tobias hesitated. "I'm preparing a broadcast. Tomorrow. It's... important."

"Another book tour?"

"No."

"Another Day of Forgiveness?"

"No. Bigger than that."

David paused. "How big?"

"Big enough that you might get calls from reporters. Maybe investigators."

"What?"

"I can't give you details. Not yet. For your protection."

"Are we in danger?"

"I don't think so. But I want you, Grandma, and Aunt Janice to be prepared. If anyone asks, tell them you're learning everything at the same time as the public."

David's tone shifted—skeptical, familiar. "Okay, Pop. Whatever you say."

Tobias sighed. "After the show, you'll understand why I couldn't say more now."

"I'll watch it," David said. "I won't tell Grandma or Aunt Janice you called. I'll make them watch with me."

"Thank you, son. Tell them I love them."

The doorbell chimed in Tobias's quarters.

The door automatically slid open, and Goren, seeing that Tobias was on the phone, telepathically apologized and indicated he would return later.

"Do you have company?" David asked.

Tobias smiled. "Something like that."

"Well, now that I know you're okay, I can breathe again."

They both laughed.

"After the show," Tobias said, "we'll talk."

"Bye, Pop."

Tobias stared at the phone after the call ended, his thoughts drifting to David as a child. So much time lost. So much still to say.

Tobias sat at the desk in his quarters, the Earth now visible through the observation window behind him. He picked up his phone and dialed Mill. She answered on the second ring.

"Toby? Is that you?"

"The one and only."

"Are you back in New York?"

"No. Still on the spaceship."

Mill paused. "You mean you've been hovering around Earth this whole time? Why didn't you call?"

"I couldn't. You wouldn't believe where I've been."

"Try me," she said, her usual sardonic tone barely masking the worry she'd carried since watching him leave.

"I bet you didn't think I'd be back so soon."

"So soon?" Mill exclaimed. "You left in late autumn. It's mid-spring."

Tobias froze. "Spring? I left just a few days ago."

Mill laughed. "Toby, it's been months. Your sister even called me three months ago, worried sick."

"You two became buddies?"

"We commiserated. I didn't spill the beans about the spaceship—she wouldn't have believed me anyway."

"You missed me, huh?"

41

"Don't get a swelled head. I nearly had to file a missing person report."

Tobias rubbed his forehead. "No wonder David sounded off. I spoke to him earlier, but I didn't pick up on it. It must be... time dilation. Einstein's theory."

Mill scoffed. "It's all Greek to me. Are you sure you didn't have one of those 'missing time' episodes?"

"No, Mill. I was awake the whole time. I was taken to another world— settled by Earth people thousands of years ago."

"What? You've got to be kidding! Wait until we tell Jimmy!"

"How is Jimmy?"

"He's fine. He's on his way over. We didn't know if you'd call. We've been running your school, giving lectures based on your books. People started asking questions. We were running out of guest speakers."

"You could've rerun an old broadcast."

"Reruns? You know we're better than that. Honestly, we just wanted to keep our spirits up. We missed you."

"*I'm* the life of the party? Mill, you jest."

"Yeah, I'm 'jest' insane to put up with all of this!"

They both laughed, the kind of laughter that only comes from years of shared struggle.

"Mill, I hope not too much has changed."

"Jimmy, Yolanda, and Grace moved into your old apartment. Now that Jimmy's nearby, he can help with the school anytime."

"That sounds great." Tobias paused. "Mill, about the upcoming broadcast…"

"Yes?"

"It's going to be one for the record books."

Just then, Mill's doorbell rang. "That must be Jimmy."

"Good. I have something important to tell both of you."

Tobias heard Jimmy's voice through the phone. "Yolanda and Grace sent this to you," he said, handing Mill a plate wrapped in plastic.

"Red velvet cake! My favorite!", Mill said. "You'll never guess who I have on the phone."

"Another disgruntled student?"

Mill put the phone on speaker.

"Can I have some of that red velvet cake too?" Tobias said.

"What? T.S.?" Jimmy exclaimed. "Do my ears deceive me?!"

"Your ears may deceive you, but it's really me."

"How've you been? Are you back?"

"I'm back, but still on the ship. I can't land until after tomorrow night's show."

"Why not?"

"You two are the only people I can tell this to." Tobias's voice cracked. "They took me to another world—settled by Earth people tens of thousands of years ago."

"What?!"

"There's more. They're afraid for us."

"Afraid of us?" Jimmy asked.

"No. Afraid *for* us. They think we're on the brink of destroying ourselves. They want to help."

"How?" Mill asked.

"They want to make their presence known. And they want to use our program to do it. I'm going to introduce an alien being to the people of Earth."

Silence.

"I guess I should've asked if you were sitting down."

"You've got that right," Mill said.

"They call their planet Jevmmuns. There's conflict over whether to contact Earth or leave us alone. They asked me to do this. I wanted to give you both a heads-up."

"How can we prepare for something like this?" Jimmy asked.

"We can't. We just brace for the reaction."

"If they take you seriously," Mill said. "You might end up on the back of a tabloid."

They laughed again, the tension breaking.

"How do you plan to do it?" Jimmy asked.

"I'll talk about humanity's potential. Then I'll introduce the extraterrestrial."

"And the rest is history," Mill said.

"One way or another," Tobias sighed. "You don't need to do anything for this week's program. Just be ready for press attention."

"Publicity is our middle name," Mill said. "Don't worry, Toby."

"The aliens will control the broadcast links. They won't land until they're sure it's safe."

"That makes sense," Mill said.

"Thanks for the heads-up, T.S.," Jimmy added.

"I need to finish the speech," Tobias said. "I must prepare."

"Try not to overdo it," Mill said.

"How can I overdo something this real?"

Silence.

Jimmy spoke. "We'll hold the fort down on this end, T.S."

"I'll contact you after the broadcast."

"We'll be watching," Mill said.

"So long," Jimmy added. "Call us if you need us."

Tobias sat at his desk, dictating the final draft of his speech. The console glowed softly, its interface intuitive and eerily responsive. He paused, staring blankly at the screen, the weight of what he was about to do pressing down on him. Slowly, he folded his arms on the desk and drifted into a restless sleep.

Then came the jolt.

The spacecraft tilted violently, throwing Tobias from his chair. He hit the floor hard, scrambled to his feet, and rushed into the corridor. As he reached the central hub, he saw the observation window—Earth was gone. Only stars and distant planets filled the void.

Stokes, Beatrice, and Goren were already there. The two Naku navigators worked silently, their hands flying across the controls.

"What happened?" Tobias asked, breathless.

Stokes turned grim. "COL followed us through the wormhole. We thought they'd only try to discourage us. We were wrong."

"Wasn't it COL who tried to stop us from landing on Jevmmuns?"

"That was a warning," Beatrice said. "This is war."

Tobias stared at her. "You sound surprised. On Earth, violence is business as usual."

Stokes nodded. "Maybe COL's Earth division corrupted the Jevmmunian branch. This is exactly why many fear contact with Earth."

Tobias turned to Goren. "Where are we now?"

Goren replied calmly, "We're in the asteroid belt. We had to flee orbit. We have no weapons."

"No weapons?" Tobias echoed, incredulous.

46

Stokes answered, "We're a peaceful mission. Violence hasn't been part of our society for centuries."

"Well, it is now," Tobias muttered.

Beatrice asked the navigators, "Are they still following?"

Goren spoke for them. "They'll find us soon. But we have a plan."

"Care to share it?" Tobias asked.

"Not yet," Goren said. "We suspect COL may be using telepathic surveillance. Human minds are easier to read than Naku minds."

Beatrice looked at Goren, surprised. "I've never heard you speak this way."

"It's not offense. It's strategy," Goren replied. "We must protect the group."

Suddenly, the COL ship appeared in the distance—flashing lights against the backdrop of motionless stars. A second blast struck the hull near the observation window. The ship lurched backward. Beatrice fell, and Tobias caught her, bracing against the railing.

"We've got to stop meeting this way," Tobias said, trying to lighten the moment.

Beatrice smiled faintly, her hand still gripping his arm.

Stokes, caught off guard and not holding the railing, hit the floor hard. Goren and the two Naku navigators remained upright, their balance unshaken as the ship veered sharply away from the asteroid belt. The sun, now just a bright star among countless others, faded behind them as the spacecraft accelerated toward the wormhole that had once carried them to Jevmmuns.

The navigators worked in perfect synchrony, their movements fluid and precise. As the ship approached the wormhole at near-light speed, they spoke— both verbally and telepathically, their voices echoing in unison.

"Hold on!"

Just before reaching the wormhole's entrance, the ship swerved at a forty-five-degree angle, narrowly avoiding entry. The pursuing COL vessel, unable to react in time, plunged into the wormhole, unaware that their target had slipped away.

Goren turned to the crew. "They've entered the wormhole. They won't be able to return for several weeks. Time distortion will delay their regrouping."

Beatrice, still gripping the handrail, exhaled. "Let's hope we can have our first contact program in peace."

"Hopefully," Stokes said, brushing himself off, his face etched with relief.

The ship turned back toward the asteroid belt, choosing to remain hidden among the drifting rocks beyond Mars. It was safer here—quiet, remote, and shielded from further interference.

Tobias returned to his quarters, the adrenaline slowly draining from his body. He lay down on his unmade bed, staring at the ceiling. The ship was calm again, but his thoughts were not.

He had called his family. He had warned his friends. He had prepared his speech. There was nothing left to do.

Let the chips fall where they may, he thought, drifting into sleep as the stars outside blinked silently, waiting for tomorrow.

Chapter 4

The Broadcast

After seven hours of restless sleep, Tobias was awakened by the soft chime of his door. It was Stokes.

"We're back in orbit around Earth," he said. "Are you ready?"

Tobias sat up, rubbing his eyes. "As ready as I'll ever be. Just give me a few minutes to change into my other silver pajamas—er, spacesuit."

Stokes chuckled. "We'll meet you outside the conference room. Only you and Goren will be inside during the broadcast."

Tobias dressed quickly, unable to eat, sipping only half a glass of something that tasted like cranberry juice. He gathered his notes and walked down the corridor, his steps slow, his mind heavy.

Beatrice stood at the entrance to the broadcast wing. She smiled warmly.

"In your culture, there's a saying when someone begins a new venture—'Break a leg.' Should I say that to you?"

Tobias smiled. "It's usually reserved for actors. But I'll take it."

She took his hand. "You'll do well. I've seen how you handle the unusual."

"I can't think of anything more unusual than this."

They shared a lingering smile. Tobias continued down the corridor.

At the conference room, Stokes and Goren waited. Tobias felt steadier now, buoyed by Beatrice's quiet confidence.

"Let's get the show on the road," he said.

Goren spoke, his voice layered with telepathic undertones. "Thank you for helping us with this monumental task. It may seem sudden, but the Council has been preparing for this moment for a long time."

Stokes added, "We just want to make sure you're comfortable."

Tobias nodded. "Comfortable? I've had my mind manipulated by an alien society. You took me to another world, and now you want me to introduce it to Earth. But yes—I'm at peace."

Stokes placed a hand on his shoulder. "You've come a long way."

"I no longer ask 'Why me?' If that helps."

Goren gestured toward the room. "It's time."

Inside, the conference table gleamed white. Tobias sat at the center, Goren at the far end. A carafe of green tea and two empty glasses sat between them. No visible cameras. No screens.

"How do I know when to begin?" Tobias asked.

"The cameras are built into the walls," Goren replied.

Tobias nodded, poured himself a glass of tea, and glanced at the mirrored monitor across the room. His image appeared—real-time, calm, composed.

He whispered to Goren, "This is it?"

Goren nodded.

Tobias looked into the monitor, took a breath, and began.

Goren's large head nodded slightly off camera, his black eyes fixed on Tobias like deep, reflective pools—beckoning attention, yet unreadable in their depth.

From the corridor, Stokes pressed the wall panel. "You're on," he said, as the door slid shut.

Tobias glanced at the closing door, then at Goren, feeling the weight of inevitability settle over him. It was like boarding a train already in motion—no turning back, only forward.

He looked into the monitor, took a breath, and began.

"Hello. Welcome to the New School of Truth program."

His voice was steady, but solemn.

"We humans have reached a pivotal point in our evolution. We are the dominant species on Earth, and we hold the greatest influence over its future. Yet, the crises we face—climate change, pollution, division, war—are all of our own making. These problems demand human-created solutions."

He paused, scanning his notes.

"Our society teaches us to believe we are alone in the universe. That we must divide ourselves into nations, cultures, ethnicities, and religions. These divisions breed conflict. And too often, we resolve those conflicts through violence."

Tobias leaned forward.

"We forget how much we share. We forget that previous civilizations— some more advanced than ours—collapsed under the weight of their own divisions. Puma Punku, for example, with its impossibly precise stonework, may be 15,000 years old. What led to its demise?"

He looked directly into the monitor.

"If we set aside our perceived differences—race, religion, gender, wealth, class, orientation, geography—we may finally progress as a species."

He glanced at Goren, who remained still, waiting.

Tobias continued.

"Human nature has always played a role in our downfall. Someone always wants to prove they're better. That their way is superior. This ideology has destroyed civilizations before. And it will destroy ours if we don't change."

He leaned forward slightly.

"How advanced are we, really, if we still threaten each other with violence and call it normal? We are an intelligent species. But how we use that intelligence will determine our fate."

He paused again, letting the silence settle.

Then, with quiet resolve, he said:

"And now, I'd like to introduce someone who will help us understand just how far our story reaches—beyond Earth, beyond history, and into the stars."

He turned to Goren.

"This is Goren, a representative of the Naku species from the planet Jevmmuns."

The camera shifted, revealing Goren's face—his large black eyes, his elongated head, his calm presence. The shot widened to show him seated beside Tobias.

"Thank you for being here, Goren," Tobias said, swiveling toward him.

"Thank you for having me," Goren replied, his voice more fluid than before.

"You're here to introduce your species to Earth."

"That is correct," Goren said. "Jevmmuns is home to both Naku and humans—humans who left Earth millennia ago."

Tobias nodded. "Why contact Earth now?"

Goren turned to the camera. "Because we fear you are on a path to self-destruction. We've seen this before—war, pollution, division. We want to help you avoid it."

"How?"

"By sharing our history. By showing how we overcame similar challenges. We believe Earth can learn from Jevmmuns."

Tobias leaned in. "How did humans end up on your planet?"

Goren replied, "About 50,000 years ago, the Naku began to incorporate humans into our society. By that time, human beings had evolved into intelligent creatures that were not very different from modern humans."

Tobias quipped, "Just give them a suit and a smartphone and let them ride the subway, and you'd never be able to tell the difference."

Goren's large eyes blinked slowly. "Indeed. The differences were subtle, but the potential was immense. We saw in early humans the capacity for empathy, creativity, and abstract thought—traits that mirrored our own evolution."

Tobias leaned forward slightly. "So you're saying this wasn't just a scientific experiment. It was a kind of... adoption?"

"In a sense," Goren said. "We did not abduct. We invited. Those who joined us did so voluntarily, often in search of peace, knowledge, or refuge from the chaos of early human societies."

Tobias nodded, absorbing the weight of that history. "And now you're inviting us again. Not physically, but philosophically."

"Exactly," Goren said. "The broadcast is not just a message. It is a mirror. We want humanity to see itself—not as fractured nations or competing ideologies, but as a single species on the brink of transformation."

Tobias turned to the camera, his voice steady. "If you're watching this, you've probably already decided whether I'm crazy, lying, or telling the truth. But I'm not here to convince you. I'm here to ask you to think. To question. To wonder."

He paused, letting the silence settle.

"Because if what Goren and the others have shown me is real—and I believe it is—then we're not alone. We never were. And maybe, just maybe, we're not as lost as we think."

The camera zoomed out slowly as Tobias and Goren sat side by side, two beings from different worlds, united by a shared hope.

Goren explained the ancient migrations, the Naku's origins on Earth, their evolution from dinosaurs, their decision to leave Earth and allow humans to evolve independently. He spoke of cave drawings, of ancient civilizations, of the long arc of human potential

Goren's small mouth formed a faint smile. Tobias hoped the humor made him seem more approachable to the audience.

But then the tone shifted.

Goren spoke of betrayal—how humans misused the New Science, how the Naku had to abandon Earth, and later Jevmmuns, to allow humanity to evolve on its own. He spoke of the Day of Reconciliation, of Greta Stokes, of the long journey toward forgiveness.

Tobias leaned back, absorbing it all.

"So your Day of Reconciliation preceded your Day of Forgiveness?"

"Yes," Goren said. "Acknowledgment, apology, forgiveness, reconciliation. That is the path."

Tobias turned to the monitor.

"I know it may sound incredulous, but I was recently able to travel to Jevmmuns and meet Greta Stokes. She's still alive. And yes, the people of Jevmmuns commonly live for hundreds of years."

He paused, then leaned forward.

"I would normally take phone calls at this point, but we've given you so much to absorb. It's best to let it sink in."

He gestured with open palms.

"Please understand—this is not a hoax. You know my books, my teachings, my efforts to bring truth into the light. This event is another truth."

He turned to Goren.

"Thank you, Goren, for appearing on the New School of Truth program."

Then back to the monitor.

"Together, let's begin a new chapter in the history of humanity."

The recessed lighting brightened. The transmission ended.

Tobias sat for a long moment, avoiding Goren's gaze.

He rubbed his face with his hands. "Did this really happen?" he asked.

"It would appear so," Goren replied.

The conference room door slid open to reveal Stokes and Beatrice standing in the doorway, both beaming. Stokes carried a bottle of what appeared to be expensive champagne from Earth.

"Congratulations to the both of you," he said, stepping inside. "I've been saving this bottle for a special occasion. The broadcast was more than we hoped for. You introduced Goren and Jevmmuns, and you laid out the stakes with clarity and heart."

Beatrice added, "Goren, your explanation of Jevmmuns' history was masterful. And Tobias—your interview format was inspired. Far better than just 'landing on the White House lawn.'"

Tobias smiled faintly. "Thank you, Beatrice."

Stokes poured champagne into four glasses. Goren, who didn't drink alcohol, filled a fifth glass with green tea and raised it with the others.

"To a job well done," Stokes said. "Let's hope this leads to bigger and better things."

They clinked glasses. Tobias sipped the champagne, its smoothness dulling his senses just enough to let the moment feel real. But beneath the surface, unease stirred. He had opened a Pandora's box. The genie was out. There was no going back.

Later, in his quarters, Tobias sat at his desk, head resting on folded arms. The champagne buzz had faded, replaced by a gnawing uncertainty. His phone chimed. He stared at it, surprised it still worked this far from Earth.

He answered.

"Well, Toby, you've outdone yourself this time!" Mill's voice rang out.

"Hi, Mill," he said, weary. "What did you think?"

"I think you've lost your mind."

Tobias blinked. "Why do you say that?"

"Did you clear this with anyone? The government? The UN?"

"You know they'd have shut it down," Tobias replied. "Besides, the crew here knows more than any Earth agency."

Mill sighed. "Well, you don't have to worry about any sudden reactions."

"Why not?"

"Because no one believes you."

Tobias sat up. "What?"

"Some former students called the school. They thought Goren was a puppet. Like Yoda. They think it was a publicity stunt for your Day of Forgiveness campaign."

Tobias groaned. "Didn't any journalists call? TV outlets?"

"Not a one."

"If Jimmy and I hadn't seen you board that ship ourselves, I'd have thought it was a hoax too," Mill said. "It's like Orson Welles all over again."

"Is Jimmy with you?"

"No, he watched it at home. Said the only thing missing was popcorn."

Tobias rubbed his temples. "I never anticipated this. I'll check with the crew—they're monitoring Earth's media."

"Don't worry, Toby," Mill said gently. "You did a good job. It'll just take time for people to catch up."

Tobias rushed to the hub. Beatrice, Goren, and Stokes were already gathered.

"What's the verdict?" he asked.

Stokes's face was unreadable. "Our celebration may have been premature. No buzz. No spikes in communication. Most viewers think it was just a new teaching method."

Tobias sighed. "Same reaction from my students. Maybe we gave them too much at once."

"Maybe," Beatrice said.

"Maybe first contact is actually a bust," Tobias muttered.

Stokes offered a reassuring smile. "At least there was no panic."

"Not yet," Tobias said. He turned to Goren. "Forgive me, but some people thought you were a puppet. A special effect."

Goren smiled faintly. "I've been called worse. Even by my own kind. They ostracized me for studying humans undercover. I wanted answers. Maybe second contact will be more effective."

"Second contact?" Tobias asked.

"I'm willing to try again. If you are."

Tobias nodded. "Sure. If that's what it'll take."

That evening, the crew met in the conference room. Tobias felt echoes of his old brainstorming sessions with Mill and Jimmy. He decided to call them after each meeting to keep them in the loop.

Beatrice opened the discussion. "Your presentation was honest. But people are used to scripted sci-fi. You were too real."

Tobias shrugged. "Just one grape in the bunch."

Goren smiled. "Yet our grape is genuine."

Stokes leaned in. "The problem was surprise. People weren't prepared. They were lulled into disbelief."

"If ever there was a lackluster response to first contact," Tobias said, "this was it."

Stokes nodded. "What's missing is a personal touch."

"A personal touch?"

"You and Goren need to interact with people in person. They need to see you. Feel you."

"How?"

"We land the spacecraft."

Everyone stared at him.

Beatrice gasped. "That would be too dangerous!"

Goren asked, "Is this what you meant by 'landing on the White House lawn'?"

"It's just an expression," Tobias said.

Stokes slammed his fist on the table. "If we're going to make first contact, let's make first contact!"

Goren added, "They can deny me. Say I'm animated. But they can't deny a ship and crew."

"With COL in retreat," Stokes said, "this may be the moment."

Beatrice asked, "Do we have Council approval?"

"They've given us discretion," Stokes replied. "Tobias and Goren can prepare the public. We'll call it 'The Great Landing.'"

"The Great Landing?" Tobias and Beatrice echoed.

"That's what the Council calls it. Got a better name?"

They all shrugged.

Tobias said, "Let's work together. Goren, should we do one or two more programs to announce our intentions?"

Goren smiled. "You read my mind. We'll make a telepath out of you yet."

The laughter from the planning session faded into quiet resolve. The crew agreed: The Great Landing would occur in a few weeks, after several more broadcasts featuring Goren. But first, Tobias would return to Earth—briefly, quietly, and anonymously.

Stokes cautioned him. "We're monitoring all communications. We'll protect you as best we can. But you won't be totally safe."

Tobias shrugged. "Who on Earth is?"

Stokes smiled wryly. "Until now, who on Jevmmuns was totally unsafe? The answer's the same—virtually no one."

"Truth," Tobias said, smiling at the crew. He walked back to his quarters, watching through the corridor windows as the ship left the asteroid belt and slipped into orbit around Earth—undetected by the planet's primitive twenty-first-century technology.

He called his son in Philadelphia. David answered quickly, his voice tinged with sarcasm.

"Pop, you really blew me away with that program. Was that really a guy from another planet?"

"You too?" Tobias sighed. "Seems no one believes it was real."

David chuckled. "C'mon, Pop. Goren looked like a cross between ET and Yoda. Is that why you disappeared? To work on a special effects project?"

Tobias's frustration boiled over. "It's not a project, David! It's real. Too real. I know I haven't been around much, but you should know me better than that."

David fell silent.

Tobias softened. "While I was away, I learned I'd been manipulated—telepathically. I'm still responsible for my absences, but it wasn't entirely my fault. I need to talk to you, your aunt, and Grandma. In person."

David hesitated. "I don't think it's a good idea right now, Pop. Ever since your broadcast, strange things have been happening."

"Like what?"

"There's a black car that keeps circling the block. A man and woman inside. They park where they can see the house."

Tobias's stomach tightened. "Go on."

"Right after the broadcast, a guy rang the doorbell. Said he was doing a political survey. Asked about you. Who lives here. If we're registered to vote. He wouldn't say what he was really after."

"Are you sure he didn't go to other houses?"

"I didn't see him knock anywhere else."

"Be on your guard, son. But don't worry."

"What can they do? We don't know anything anyway."

"That makes two of us," Tobias said, and they both laughed nervously.

"I'll see you soon. Love you, boy."

"We love you too, Pop."

They hung up. Tobias sat in silence, then called Mill.

She answered after four rings, her voice hesitant.

"Hi, Toby."

"Hi, Mill. Is there any place on Earth where I can rest my weary head?"

Mill didn't laugh. She was silent.

"I'm heading home soon. Can't stay at my old place—Jimmy and his family live there now. My family's under surveillance. That leaves you."

"Uh, Toby… let me call you back in a little while," she said, almost meekly.

"Sure, Mill. No problem."

Tobias was puzzled. Her voice lacked its usual edge. Mill had always been the fortress—blunt, feisty, unflinching. They'd met in law school, bonded over their shared outsider status. Tobias used wit to shield his vulnerability; Mill used toughness to defend hers. They were opposites in temperament but identical in pain—two people who had learned to navigate the world with armor stitched from rejection. Mill, short, pale, and heavy, and Tobias, tall, slender, and brown, had been an unlikely pair for decades. They were like siblings—unapologetically "us against the world." Both had known the sting of ostracism. Both had learned to survive by leaning on each other.

He stretched out on his bed, the spaceship still orbiting Earth. He waited for her call, but it didn't come. Not that night.

Chapter 5

Descent Into Spring

Mill didn't call until the next day.

The phone chimed. Tobias answered on the second ring.

"Is everything okay?" he asked.

"I'm fine," she said, trying to sound casual.

"What's up?"

"I've been meaning to tell you… Phillip contacted me."

"Phillip? Your ex-husband?"

Mill's voice was quiet. "Yes. I guess I've told you something about him."

Tobias raised his voice slightly. "You sure did—and then some. Didn't you say you were done with him? Wasn't his temper and violent behavior the reason you divorced him?"

"That was a long time ago," she said. "Before you and I met. Before law school. People change."

"But Phillip?"

Mill's tone remained serious. "Over the past year, Tobias, you weren't around much. Long before you left on the spaceship, you'd already left us on Earth. You focused on work. You stopped seeing Jimmy and me. You made it clear we had to give you space."

She paused. "Phillip came back and partially filled that space. He stopped by last night—right before you called."

"You didn't sound very happy on the phone."

"I've never been happy around him," she said. "Too much water under the bridge."

"Then why let him visit?"

Mill hesitated. "I was lonely. I didn't want to bother Jimmy and his family. There were no big problems at the school. And… I missed you, Toby. Dare I say that without giving you a swelled head?"

Tobias smiled, relieved. "Nothing could swell my head after what I've been through. Only you and Jimmy can really understand."

"Do you feel safe around Phillip?" he asked gently.

"I think time and maturity have played their role. He's older now. Not as quick-tempered. And I'm older too—and I won't put up with any guff from him."

She paused again. "But there's something strange…"

"Yes?"

"I hadn't seen him in years. Then, out of nowhere, he contacted me about six months ago—when I was alone, and you and Jimmy were doing your own things. It was almost like he knew it was a good time to reconnect."

"And you were a willing party?"

65

"I guess so, Toby. But now I may be in too deep. A lot of bad memories are cropping up. I don't know if I want to fully reconnect. He hurt me badly—physically and mentally."

Tobias spoke softly. "Mill, I'm no therapist, but maybe you let him back in because you needed closure."

"Maybe. Or maybe I was just trying to fill a void."

"Would any of this interfere with me staying with you for a few days before my next program? This might be my last chance to come back to Earth for a while."

"If it's like the first broadcast, Toby, you'll have nothing to worry about," she quipped. "Of course you can stay here. You're always welcome. And if Phillip comes around, it'd be good for him to see I'm not totally alone."

Mill remembered how, years ago, Phillip had become increasingly abusive when he realized she had no family and few friends to protect her. Her isolation had emboldened him. Tobias's presence now offered a quiet shield.

"Thanks, Mill," Tobias said. "I should be there tomorrow. Maybe I'll go to Philadelphia for a day if the coast is clear."

"Then back to the spaceship?"

"That's the plan. I'll interview Goren again. We'll see how the world responds."

"Are you sure you want to go through with this?"

"I've never been more certain of anything in my life."

"Then I'll see you tomorrow, my dear."

"Bye, Mill. And thanks again."

Tobias sat up and left his quarters, keeping the sliding door open. He walked down the corridor toward the hub of the ship and saw the two Naku navigators busy at the controls, monitoring the array of dials, screens, lights, and buttons.

As he approached the navigators, Tobias smiled. "Don't you guys ever sleep?" he asked half-jokingly.

As usual, the two Naku pilots, who always seemed to be able to shield their telepathic thoughts from Tobias, formed the slit of their mouths into a semblance of a smile, and simultaneously nodded their heads as a form of acknowledgment. They then returned to their work without telepathically or verbally answering Tobias's question.

Stokes, entering the hub from an adjacent corridor, approached.

"The Naku require relatively little sleep as compared to us humans, Tobias. Isn't it most obscene that we should waste eight hours each day in slumber?" asked Stokes.

Tobias, both surprised and amused, responded, "You seem to be up most of the time yourself, Stokes. Are you sure that you are not part-Naku yourself?" They both laughed lightly, while the two Naku pilots remained busy with the ship.

Stokes and Tobias reached the corridor outside the conference room, but instead of entering, Stokes reached up into an open panel embedded in the wall. From it, he retrieved a thin silver chain holding a black and silver medallion. He held it out to Tobias.

"During your stay on Earth," said Stokes, "it would be useful for you to wear this device around your neck. It'll let us monitor you—for your safety—and you can contact us if anything unexpected happens."

Tobias took the medallion, examining its pyramid-like shape with smooth, rounded edges. The front was etched with a combination of Mayan glyphs and Egyptian hieroglyphics; the back held a small button carved in the shape of an Egyptian ankh.

He smirked. "Can I use it to tell you I've fallen, and I can't get up?"

Stokes blinked, missing the reference entirely. "We don't anticipate any issues. Your visit to Earth should be uneventful. We'd like to rendezvous back at the upstate clearing in about seventy-two hours."

Tobias tucked the medallion beneath his shirt. "Okay. So I'll return to the ship Monday morning. The second broadcast with Goren goes live on Wednesday—just enough time to prepare."

"Why not come back Sunday night instead?" said Stokes. "Say, eight o'clock? That way you won't have to drive overnight."

"Good idea," Tobias nodded.

"I'll also be on Earth during that time," said Stokes, "but I'll be stationed elsewhere."

"I always wondered where you stayed during those book tours," Tobias said. "You seemed to shadow me in every city."

Stokes grinned. "That's my secret."

Tobias admired the medallion once more. "Nice piece of jewelry."

"It's a communication device," Stokes replied. "Press the button on the back if you need anything."

Tobias smiled. "Let's get the show on the road. I'm packed and ready."

Stokes spoke to the Naku pilots. The ship dropped from its orbit and glided silently toward the same secluded clearing near the Canadian border—the place where this strange journey had begun. The descent was swift. Tobias barely had time to retrieve his bag before arriving at the exit ramp.

At the window, he noticed something peculiar: the bare trees of late autumn were now vibrant and leafy. The terrain below was lush, bursting with mid-spring vegetation.

Mill was right, he thought. More than five months have passed.

"Yes," said Goren, both verbally and telepathically. "You missed the entire winter and early spring."

"Lucky me," Tobias muttered, unable to hide his mild annoyance at the invasion of thought.

Goren replied, telepathically and gently: Forgive me for reading your thoughts. I see you as a friend and took the liberty of teasing you.

To his own surprise, Tobias responded telepathically: No offense taken. I see you as a friend too. You've taught me to focus my thoughts. I hope I've helped you feel more at ease speaking aloud.

Goren nodded. "Indeed you have. Enjoy your visit to Earth."

Beatrice stepped forward and took Tobias's hand in both of hers. "I hope you enjoyed Jevmmuns. I'm looking forward to your return."

"You made my maiden voyage quite agreeable," he said.

They exchanged a smile layered with meaning. Then the exit ramp unfurled and touched the ground. The two Naku pilots sent their silent farewells, nodding and sending telepathic well wishes.

"I'm leaving too," said Stokes. "But we'll travel separately."

Tobias paused midway down the ramp, then turned. "So long, everyone. See you in a few days."

Beatrice and Goren waved as the ship's ramp retracted and the door slid shut. The spacecraft shot skyward, vanishing into the bright spring horizon.

Tobias and Stokes stood alone in the quiet clearing, surrounded by tall pines. Two Mercedes-Benz cars waited in the shadows—one black, one silver.

Tobias turned to Stokes. "How did you manage to have cars waiting in such a remote place?"

"Just as COL has agents on Earth, so does the Council," said Stokes. "You were curious about my whereabouts—I meet regularly with our Earth-based members. They handled the logistics."

"Can I meet them?"

"Not yet. The Council wants to stay incognito. Especially if COL is watching."

Tobias gestured toward the vehicles. "Which one should I take?"

"Your choice—black or silver."

"I'll take the black. Better to be inconspicuous."

"Both are GPS-equipped. Follow me until we reach the New York State Thruway. You'll head down to New York City, and I'll make some stops in the Hudson Valley."

"Sounds good," Tobias said. "Call me if you want to grab a bite on the way. I could go for a deli sandwich, after all this time."

"We'll make it happen," said Stokes, climbing into the silver coupe.

Tobias entered the black car and settled in. He was eager to begin this seventy-two-hour reprieve, though part of him knew reprieve was too generous a term.

Stokes pulled away first, heading down the dirt road beside an abandoned farm. Weeds swayed against wild barley and wheat. Grasshoppers landed briefly on both windshields. The GPS in Tobias's car struggled to locate their position.

Recalculating. Recalculating.

Tobias followed Stokes well past the quiet backroads. By the time they reached the busier highway, the GPS voice had regained its composure, now reflecting every turn Stokes made with cheerful precision.

Halfway to the New York State Thruway, they stopped at a fast-food delicatessen and ordered submarine sandwiches. The restaurant was nearly empty. As they sat at a small table, Stokes leaned in.

"Where do you plan to go first?"

"I'm staying with Mill in Brooklyn tonight," Tobias said. "Then I'll head to Philadelphia to see my family."

Stokes raised an eyebrow. "That's a lot to pack into three days."

"Don't worry. I'll be back in time for the rendezvous Sunday night. Just think of it as a whirlwind weekend."

"I've never had one of those," Stokes said. "Life on Jevmmuns is so relaxed, we don't need weekends. Every day is like a weekend."

"Don't you get bored?"

"Never. We focus on mental and spiritual growth. No armies. No borders. No energy wasted on defending ourselves from each other."

Tobias nodded. "No wonder Jevmmuns sees Earth as primitive."

"Primitive is such a harsh word," Stokes said.

"Harsh but accurate."

They both laughed. Then, quietly, they returned to their cars and continued south. Two hours north of New York City, Stokes called Tobias on his hands-free phone.

"I'm taking the next exit. I won't be far. Call me if you need anything."

"Thanks, Stokes. I'll be okay. This'll be the first time I've been truly alone since I left Earth. I hope I can handle it."

"You'll be fine," Stokes said. "Piece of cake."

Stokes rolled down his window and waved. Tobias beeped his horn lightly and continued toward Brooklyn.

It was late afternoon when Tobias arrived in Brooklyn. He turned onto Mill's block, almost driving past it out of habit, as if his old apartment were still waiting for him. The city looked the same—busy and quiet at once.

He parked around the corner, grabbed his bag, and walked briskly toward Mill's building. People passed by—walking dogs, returning from work, living their lives. The days of lockdown and distancing were long gone. A new normal had settled in.

Tobias inhaled deeply. The smells, the sounds, the energy—it all felt familiar. Like returning from a long book tour. In his mind, he'd only been gone a week.

Mill's building was a modest four-story sandstone walkup nestled among brownstones on a tree-lined street. He rang the bell. She buzzed him in. Her apartment was on the second floor.

As he reached the top of the stairs, Mill flung open the door and smiled broadly. They hugged and kissed each other on the cheeks.

"You really did a number on all of us, Toby!"

"This whole experience has done a number on me," he said. "You wouldn't believe what I've been through."

"Try me," she said with her familiar smirk, ushering him inside.

Her apartment was warm, eclectic, and unmistakably hers. Soft textures, floral upholstery, tapestries from faraway places. Brass chimes, stone fountains, wooden beads. Books everywhere—on tables, chairs, shelves. It was less a space for guests and more a sanctuary for Mill herself.

The living room's bay window filtered the early evening light through pastel curtains. A spring breeze stirred the fabric. Aromas from the kitchen—carrots, spices, broth—drifted into the room.

Tobias settled into his usual spot: a maroon easy chair across from Mill's habitual seat on the sofa. They were like an old married couple—routines, rituals, unspoken rhythms.

Mill smiled, taking in the moment. "So, what's going on?"

"We're moving forward with first contact," Tobias said. "The first program was just the beginning."

Mill's face turned skeptical. "The beginning of what? Toby, there are UFO shows everywhere. What makes your program different?"

"It's different," Tobias said, "because we're going to land on the White House lawn—so to speak."

Mill blinked. "What?"

"I'm working with real extraterrestrial beings, Mill. Human and nonhuman. They're planning something called the 'Great Landing,' and they want me to help bring their message to Earth."

Mill stared at him. "After five months of Jimmy and me covering for you, running reruns, making excuses… you're telling me you're part of an alien invasion?"

"No, Mill. It's not an invasion. They want to help."

She laughed. "Sure they do. Remember that old *Twilight Zone* episode? The aliens said they came to help us—and then served us up for dinner."

Tobias chuckled. "*To Serve Man*. Don't worry, Mill. We wouldn't taste good anyway. We're too old and tough."

"Speak for yourself, Toby!"

The soup on the stove began to boil over. Mill rushed to the kitchen, and Tobias followed. The aroma of carrots and ginger filled the air.

"What's going on with Jimmy?" Tobias asked.

"He's running the school well. Teaching a course on the New Science based on your books. I mostly handle admin and legal stuff now."

"He's come a long way," Tobias said, remembering the aimless college student he'd once hired—pregnant girlfriend in tow.

Mill ladled soup into a bowl and handed it to Tobias with crackers on the side. "Want to surprise Jimmy after dinner? You'll be amazed at how much Grace has grown."

They sat at the dinette table, sipping soup and reconnecting. Though not biologically related, Tobias and Mill had become surrogate grandparents to Grace.

Jimmy and Yolanda had met in foster care, and Tobias and Mill had filled the void of family.

They talked until dusk. Mill updated Tobias on the usual strife, warfare, and political turmoil. Tobias shared what he'd learned about Jevmmuns, COL, and the Council. Mill, as always, took it in stride.

Before it got too late, Mill called Jimmy.

"Come on over," Jimmy said. "You're always welcome."

Tobias left his bag in Mill's second bedroom—a cozy den filled with exotic art, brass statues, incense burners, and a convertible sofa atop an ornate Oriental rug.

He looked around and quipped, "Mill, I'm going to wake up in a land far, far away."

Mill smiled from the doorway. "This room has a vibe. Perfect for yoga and meditation. You should try it."

"Maybe I will. But I'll still be far, far away."

They walked together to Jimmy and Yolanda's apartment, just a few blocks away. As Tobias walked, unease crept in. He was returning to the place where he'd once abandoned his family and career in pursuit of a half-understood dream. Now, knowing the Jevmmunians had manipulated him, anger and bitterness resurfaced. He wanted to tell Mill—but couldn't. Not yet.

At the apartment building, Mill led the way. Tobias stayed behind, out of view of the peephole. She rang the doorbell. A melodious chime echoed inside.

Jimmy opened the door and saw Tobias behind Mill.

"Oh, Mill. You really got me this time!"

He hugged Tobias tightly, laughing and crying. Then he stepped back, holding Tobias at arm's length.

"You look good, T.S.," Jimmy said, using Tobias's initials.

"So do you, Jimmy. Holding down the fort?"

"I'm doing my best. Come in, you guys."

Jimmy stepped aside, letting Mill and Tobias enter the apartment. Tobias paused, momentarily disoriented. Though he'd lived there for over three years, the space felt unfamiliar—bright, cheerful, and alive, as if it were still mid-afternoon. When he'd lived there, it had always felt dim, hollow, and bleak.

Grace, now a three-year-old toddler, ran up to Mill. "Grandma!" she squealed.

Mill bent down and kissed her cheek. "Hi, my little angel."

Tobias watched, struck by how much Grace had grown. She looked at him and smiled politely, vaguely recognizing him as someone kind. The absence of a few months had erased her memory of him as "Grandpa."

Yolanda entered from the kitchen, greeted Mill, and then hugged Tobias, insisting he stay seated. She had long respected him, and only recently felt comfortable calling him by his first name.

"Tobias," she said, "I never got to thank you for letting us stay here."

She glanced at Jimmy, who now held Grace on his lap. The child was drifting into sleep.

"While you were away," Yolanda continued, "Jimmy talked about you every day. He won't admit it, but he was worried."

"We all were," Mill added.

Tobias smiled awkwardly. "Don't worry. I'm still in one piece." He quickly changed the subject, uncomfortable with concern.

"Yolanda, you and Jimmy have really turned this place into a home."

He scanned the room—yellow curtains, matching placemats, a bowl of dried ambrosia on a curio table. It was warm, lived-in. When he'd lived there, it had felt like a waiting room for a life that never arrived.

"T.S.," Jimmy said, "I had to tell Yolanda where you'd gone. Otherwise, she'd wonder why you gave us the apartment and why I was always at the school."

Yolanda laughed. "You've got that right, my love." She kissed Jimmy, picked up the sleeping Grace, and carried her to bed.

"Don't worry, Tobias," she said over her shoulder. "Your secret's safe with me."

"It's okay," Tobias replied. "It's not a secret anymore."

Jimmy pulled up a chair, sat backward on it, and rested his chin on the backrest.

"So, what's the scoop?"

"In a nutshell, I'm only on Earth for a couple of days," Tobias said. "I'm seeing my family in Philly tomorrow, then heading back to the ship to move forward with first contact."

"You're bringing that extraterrestrial guy back on the program?"

"Yes. His name is Goren. He's from Jevmmuns—but his roots are Earth-based. He's actually a dinosaur."

"A dinosaur?!" Jimmy and Mill exclaimed in unison.

"Yes. It's a long story. But the point is, we need to help people understand Jevmmuns and its connection to Earth."

Jimmy looked skeptical. "T.S., people are going to think it's entertainment. You'll need more than a movie-style alien to convince them."

"Believe me, Jimmy, you can't fake this."

"Even I had trouble believing Goren was real," Jimmy admitted. "And I saw you take off on the spaceship!"

Mill jumped in. "Nothing fazes me when it comes to you, Toby. But Jimmy's right. The program was so unbelievable, no one was shocked—or convinced."

"I'm not trying to shock anyone," Tobias said. "We're trying to show there's a better way forward. The people of Jevmmuns want to help us avoid self-destruction."

"Then say it!" Mill exclaimed. "Yell it from the rooftops!" She smirked. "And what's this *'we'* stuff? Are you from Jevmmuns now too?"

Tobias chuckled. "They do kind of grow on you."

Yolanda returned to the living room. "Let me in on the joke."

"We were brainstorming," Jimmy said.

"Sounded like old times," she said. "What's the topic?"

"Making the program seem more realistic," Jimmy said. "Remember what I said during the broadcast?"

Yolanda nodded. "You said the alien didn't look real. It all seemed too bizarre."

Tobias smiled at her. "Any suggestions? You came up with the Day of Forgiveness campaign."

Yolanda thought for a moment. "If there are humans on Jevmmuns, why not have one of them on the program? It would feel less like science fiction and more like a conversation."

"Sure," Mill said. "Either they'll think you dragged in a deluded person off the street—or you've got the real McCoy."

Tobias's eyes lit up. "I think you've got something there, Yolanda!"

"Does it really only take a human to reach another human?" Jimmy asked.

"Yes! Exactly!" Tobias said. "Each one reach one, each one teach one. Instead of shocking people with an alien, we introduce the idea through a human. And I know the perfect person—she's from Jevmmuns and an expert on their history and ties to Earth."

"Who is that?" asked Mill.

"Her name is Beatrice," Tobias said. "She's one of the crew members on the ship. She gave me a crash course in Jevmmunian history. I'll ask her when I return."

He felt the glow of collaboration again—of working with friends, not just surviving. "Once more, you guys have come through for me."

The four of them spent the rest of the evening sharing wine, laughter, and ideas. But mostly, they basked in the comfort of each other's company. Tobias was back, if only briefly, and that was enough.

After midnight, Tobias and Mill walked home together. The Brooklyn streets were quiet, the air cool. As they approached Mill's building, a shadowy figure paced near the entrance.

Mill stiffened. "Phillip," she whispered.

He was a husky man with a thick mustache, his posture tense and irritated. As they approached, Phillip stared at Tobias but spoke to Mill.

"I needed to see you, Mill. But now I see why I had to wait."

His voice was suspicious, echoing the bitterness of their final days together. Mill hadn't heard that tone in years.

"Phillip," she said calmly. "This is my friend, Tobias."

Tobias extended a hand. "Phillip, I'm glad to meet yo—"

"I know who you are," Phillip growled. "I've been keeping up with your books and programs." He turned to Mill but spoke to Tobias. "I see you've dragged Mill into your world. She's always loved things that can't love her back."

Mill and Tobias exchanged a stunned glance. Phillip, seeing their reaction, reined himself in. He offered no apology.

"I guess I'm just edgy from waiting too long," he muttered. Then, turning to Mill, "What I needed to talk about can wait until tomorrow."

He stared at them briefly, then walked off into the night.

Mill's voice hardened. "Can you believe I was married to that guy for almost four years?"

Tobias sighed. "How did you take it?"

"One drop at a time. He still needs fixing."

"You could say that again."

They entered Mill's apartment without saying another word. Exhausted from the reunion, the wine, and the confrontation, they wished each other good night and collapsed into their respective beds.

Tobias slept deeply, undisturbed until late morning. He awoke to the smell of pancakes and coffee, and the gentle chimes swaying in the spring breeze from the open kitchen window.

He dressed quickly and entered the kitchen.

"Now I know this is a special occasion," he said. "You haven't made pancakes since law school."

Mill chuckled. "We needed a pick-me-up back then."

They sat at the table. Tobias poured coffee while Mill placed a stack of pancakes and plant-based sausages on the table.

"Thanks for putting me up," Tobias said. "I need to get an early start to see my folks in Philly."

"Pretty big day, huh?"

"It's been months since I've seen them. I didn't expect time to pass so quickly."

"None of us did," she said, then paused. "How's David?"

"He sounds okay on the phone, but I need to see him. He doesn't know what to make of my topsy-turvy life."

Mill stirred her coffee. "Phillip came back into my life out of nowhere. I can see why I divorced him."

"Is he getting violent again?"

"No. But I see the potential. He hasn't changed much. I've got to cut him loose. Again."

"Yeah, Mill. It's no use trying to get water from a dry well."

Tobias checked his watch. "I've got to get cracking. Saturday traffic can be worse than weekdays."

"Be careful, Toby."

Chapter 6

Home Again

Tobias hit the road. He'd made the trip many times by train, but this was his first time driving in years. The GPS was more helpful than expected—he couldn't remember the route.

He thought of his mother, sister, and son. *I'm going to fix it,* he told himself. *It wasn't my fault.*

He reached Philadelphia by early afternoon, crossed the Benjamin Franklin Bridge, and drove through Center City. The memories came flooding back—his youth, his roots.

He parked at the end of his old block near Temple University and walked toward his family's row house. The porch paint was peeling. The house had seen better days—brighter days, when his father was still alive.

He looked up and down the block. No black cars. No watchers. Just the quiet hum of a neighborhood that hadn't changed much, even as he had.

Tobias hesitated at the door. He didn't use his key. Instead, he pressed the doorbell and waited on the porch for more than a minute.

Janice opened the door. Normally, she would've greeted him with mock surprise and a teasing jab about his long absence. But after five months of silence, she showed only relief. Her smooth brown face was etched with new lines—worry lines. She had been caring for their mother, Rebecca, and helping guide her nephew, David. The stress had taken its toll. She'd even taken a leave of absence from her job as a social worker.

"Tobias?" she asked, disbelief in her eyes. She grabbed him and hugged him tightly, sobbing into his shoulder. "You scared us half to death!"

Tobias's own eyes glistened. "I didn't mean to worry you. It couldn't be helped."

They entered the house and stood in the vestibule. Janice closed the door and turned to him.

"We had no idea what was going on," she said, her voice rising. "Momma, David, and I saw your last program together. Do you really expect us to believe you were on another planet with that ET-looking creature? I know you're trying to promote your books, but don't you think you've gone too far?"

"Janice, you don't understand," Tobias said gently. "The program was real."

She stepped back, then walked into the larger foyer. Tobias followed her into the kitchen, where several half-full grocery bags sat on the table. He pulled out a chair and began helping her unpack.

"Tobias, we need you," she said, her voice softening. "Momma may need to switch apartments with me. She can't manage the stairs anymore. But you're off playing publicity games and forgetting your family. We don't have time for puppets or special effects, little brother. I'm glad you're okay—but we've got real problems."

"I'll say it again, Janice: the program was real. I went to another planet."

Janice stared at him. "You've become a laughingstock around here. And you've sent David into a tailspin. He doesn't know which way is up."

"I didn't mean to disappear. Mill didn't know everything either."

Janice paused. "What did she know?"

"She knew I went away on a spaceship. She was sworn to secrecy."

"You mean to tell me you really left Earth? And you couldn't tell us?"

"What would you have done if Mill told you I was in outer space? You'd have called the police. You'd have thought something terrible happened."

Janice's anger began to fade. "You're right. We would've left no stone unturned."

She looked at him, finally beginning to understand. "Tobias? Are you saying the program was real?"

"There's more," Tobias said, taking her hand. "I wasn't entirely responsible for my behavior these past few years. The extraterrestrials manipulated my mind. They made me leave my law career and my family. My books were real—but I was used."

Janice was still skeptical. "So ET made you turn your back on us?"

"I know you're angry, Sis. But it wasn't my fault."

Janice sighed. "Don't worry about me or Mom. Worry about David."

"What's wrong with David?"

"He stays to himself. Doesn't have many friends. Remember when he used to be so headstrong?"

"Yes," Tobias said, smiling. "When he was attacked on my program for being gay, he stood his ground. 'You don't tell me—I tell you!'"

They both laughed, remembering the boy who had stretched his wings.

Janice's tone grew serious. "He's not like that anymore. He's withdrawn. Quiet. I think he felt abandoned when you left."

Tobias said nothing. He knew he'd failed as a father. *Damn those Jevmmunians,* he thought. *I'm going to fix this. I'm going to fix us.*

"David works at a nursing home," Janice continued. "He's with art and music therapists. But mostly, he reads and stays in his room. Something changed in him when you left."

"I'll speak with him. He can't keep it all bottled up."

"How long will you be here?"

"Just tonight and tomorrow," Tobias said. "I have to finish what I started."

Janice looked doubtful. "Are you going back to that other planet?"

"No, Sis. I'm going to work on you Earthlings first."

They laughed as they finished putting away the groceries.

"Well, it's time for me to go upstairs and surprise Mom," Tobias said.

Janice looked up at him. "She's not quite the same. Her dementia is getting worse. She doesn't speak much. She's unsteady. You'll see."

Tobias felt a sting of guilt as they climbed the stairs. Janice opened the door to their mother's living room—the space where Tobias, Janice, and their estranged brother Willie had grown up.

Rebecca sat in her easy chair, facing the TV, watching her usual home shopping channel. She rarely bought anything, but she was still fascinated by the displays—like window shopping on a busy Philadelphia street.

Tobias remembered those childhood outings with his mother. Department stores, boutiques, and finally, a hot dog with mustard, an orange soda, and a slice of chocolate cream pie at the luncheonette. It was their special time.

He stared at her elderly profile, still lit with that same gleam in her eyes.

He stepped behind her chair, wrapped his arms around her shoulders, and kissed her cheek. "Hi, Mom," he said softly.

"Tobias?" she said, tears streaming down her face. "The Lord has answered my prayers! Boy, where have you been?"

They hugged and rocked together as she whispered, "Thank you, Jesus."

Rebecca was never excessively pious—except during moments like this.

Tobias cried as he slowly released his embrace, pulling up a dining chair beside his mother's easy chair. Janice stood near the door, beaming at the reunion. She turned toward the kitchen. "Momma, you're not going to believe this."

Tobias held his mother's hands. "Mom, I didn't mean to stay away so long, but... I kind of lost track of time." He felt like a teenager again, trying to explain why he'd come home late. But this time, the forgiveness he hoped for didn't come.

Rebecca stared blankly. "I sometimes lose track of time too, Tobias. How long have you been gone?"

Tobias's heart sank. Her once-sharp mind was clouded by dementia. She knew he'd been gone longer than usual, but something was missing. The mother he'd known wasn't fully there.

He slowed his speech. "To me, it's been just a few days. But to you, it may feel like months."

"Does being a lawyer take you away from home that much?" she asked, forgetting he'd left his law career years ago.

"No," he said softly, tears welling again. "I've been traveling. I'm sorry it's been so long."

They hugged again. Tobias promised her—and himself—that he would make things right. He was in control of his mind again. He believed in a fresh start.

Janice returned with a tray of food. "No need to go into the kitchen, Momma. You and Tobias should keep talking. This is a special occasion."

She placed a plate of roasted chicken, vegetables, and brown rice in front of their mother, along with a glass of iced tea.

"Tobias, there's plenty of chicken. Go on in the kitchen and bring back a couple trays for us…" She grinned. "If you please."

Tobias set up the trays. Janice brought in two more plates. The three of them sat around the TV, watching the home shopping channel and eating together. They kept the conversation light, avoiding talk of outer space or Tobias's absence. He followed Janice's lead, asking his mother about the items on screen.

As afternoon turned to evening, Janice found some classic pop and soul CDs. She played them on the old stereo. Motown filled the room—the soundtrack of their childhood. Rebecca's spirit brightened. The living room felt like old times.

By nightfall, Tobias and Janice were dancing in front of their mother, pretending to be on Soul Train. All three were laughing, telling stories from when the house was vibrant and alive.

None of them heard David's key in the lock.

He stood in the doorway, jeans and guitar slung over his shoulder, canvas bag in hand. Tobias spun toward him mid-dance.

"David!" he exclaimed, rushing to hug his son.

David stood stiffly, not hugging back. Tobias stopped smiling. He pulled back, searching David's eyes. David looked away, hiding resentment and hurt.

Janice turned down the music. Rebecca kept watching TV.

Tobias glanced at Janice, remembering her advice.

"I guess we have a lot to talk about, son," Tobias said.

"I guess," David replied, staring at the floor.

Janice tried to break the ice. "Hey, David. I made some chicken. You can fix a plate when you're ready."

"Thanks, Auntie, but I ate at the nursing home."

"I hope it was good," she said, heading to the kitchen to wash dishes.

David called into the living room. "Hi, Grandma."

"Hi, sweetheart," she replied.

David looked at his father. "Pop, I've got to put these things down. Want to come to my room?"

"Sure," Tobias said, admiring the guitar. "How long have you been playing?"

"For a while now," David replied curtly, walking toward his room.

Tobias followed. "Excuse me, Mom," he said, but Rebecca didn't hear him—entranced by the shopping channel.

David's room hadn't changed much. It was the same room Tobias once shared with his brother Willie. Now it was David's. Music-themed posters and photos adorned the walls. A black-and-white image of Billie Holiday hung near the bed—somber, elegant, iconic.

"Come in, Pop," David said, motioning him inside.

Tobias stepped in, smiling faintly at the memories. David sat on the bed, cradling his guitar. Tobias took the easy chair in the corner.

"David," he said, voice heavy with regret and love. "I know I haven't been a good father. I've been missing in action most of your life. The last few years have been rough. I still had to make a living for us."

"For *us*, Pop?" David snapped, unable to look at him. "You left us for a whole new life in New York. It didn't feel like there was an 'us' involved."

Tobias sighed. "I deserve that."

David continued. "First, you and Mom got divorced when I was so young I barely remember when we were all together. Then I had to get used to living only with her, and I had to be happy seeing you just a couple times a month."

Tobias nodded, silent, letting David speak.

"Then when Mom was killed, you brought me here to live. You were here, but not really here. It was like my father was a ghost, and I had to fend for myself. I was only fourteen, Pop! *Fourteen!* By the time you left for New York four years later, it was like you'd already been gone long before you actually left. And then when you called me five months ago and said you were leaving New York and didn't know where you were going—I kind of gave up on you."

Tobias shook his head. "No, son. Don't give up on me. I haven't given up on *you*. I know I left abruptly, but it couldn't be helped. I didn't know time would pass so quickly on Earth while I was away."

David looked at him, angry and skeptical. "You said on your program that you went away on a spaceship. That you went to another planet? Pop, how can you expect me to believe that?"

Tears began to roll down David's cheeks.

"You should know I wouldn't lie to you," Tobias said, his own eyes glistening. "While I was away, I learned I was being manipulated—telepathically. I wasn't fully responsible for my actions. They made me leave my career and my family. They said it was for the greater good of Earth."

"I don't care!" David exploded. He stood up, dropping his guitar on the floor. "All I know is you left us to fend for ourselves! You abandoned me! You abandoned *us*! How could you, Pop? How could you!"

He collapsed back onto the bed, sobbing. Tobias reached over and rubbed his back.

"I'm sorry, son. I'm so sorry," he said. "I didn't know what I was doing. I'll try my best to make it up to you. We can start fresh."

Tobias hugged David from behind, resting his head gently on his son's back.

"I promise you—I'll do much better."

David's body slowly relaxed. Tobias sat up, knowing there wasn't much more he could say. He made a vow to himself, to David, and to God: his actions would speak louder than his words.

"Don't worry, son. You'll see."

David sat up, wiping his face. Tobias looked around the room, admiring the musical theme.

"I like what you've done here," he said, pointing to the Billie Holiday poster. "She was popular even before my time. I know she died before I was born."

"I know she struggled," David said quietly. "Just like I'm struggling."

"She struggled with drugs and racism," Tobias said. "Are you dealing with those?"

"No, Pop. I'm not using drugs. My struggle is with my own mind. But the end result feels the same. Sometimes I feel like she does in that poster—sad, alone, forgotten."

David picked up his guitar. His mood began to brighten. Tobias sensed him relaxing.

"Your aunt told me you're working with music therapists in a nursing home. Thinking of making a career out of it?"

"Music helps me forget the sadness. It lifts my spirit when nothing else can. You should see how it helps the seniors. I play guitar and sing for them. Sometimes they sing along."

"What do you sing?"

"Old tunes. Motown. Like the ones you were dancing to tonight." David teased him. "But mostly I write my own songs. They seem to like it."

"Can I hear one?"

"Sure, Pop."

David strummed a gentle, somber melody. Tobias listened, transfixed, as the lyrics unfolded:

It's sad that I have come up to the point

In my life

Where the dreams and hopes and the desires

Aren't in sight

Where the sweet melodies

Blend with cold memories

To make the path that I will call

My destiny

No one ever tried for me

No one ever lied for me

No one ever touched that special core

Deep inside

No one ever cried for me

No one ever sighed for me

No one ever felt the tenderness

I can't hide

Paul Anthony

I now must find what lies behind the bend

In my life

One wrong step can mean a certain end

One long night

Can my feelings show

That I love you so

For then you will realize

And you'll know

No one ever tried for me

No one ever lied for me

No one ever touched that special core

Deep inside

No one ever cried for me

No one ever sighed for me

No one ever felt the tenderness

I can't hide

The room was silent. Tobias looked down at the rug, then up at his son.

"Is that how you really feel?"

"Sometimes," David said, cradling his guitar.

"Is there someone special in your life?"

"No. Not at the moment. But the song wasn't just about romance, Pop."

"I know," Tobias said. "I just regret that you had to feel such pain. Don't worry, son. I'll try for you."

They stood and finally hugged—wiping away a lifetime of pain and resentment. They talked past midnight. About childhood. About guilt. About hope. For the first time, they truly listened.

Tobias yawned. "I'm going to bed. I'll be in your Aunt Janice's old room. Good night, son."

"You too, Pop."

Tobias walked to the door. "And David," he said, smiling, "Try to write some happier tunes."

David smiled. "Will do, Pop. Will do."

Tobias checked on his mother—asleep. Janice had gone downstairs. He turned off the TV, dimmed the lights, and entered Janice's old room.

It hadn't changed much. He remembered long talks, her departure, her return. Now it was a guest room. He scanned the room, feeling warmth.

There's a history here, he thought. *My history.*

He climbed into bed and slept well, knowing he'd begun to help heal his broken family.

Chapter 7

The Great Landing

Tobias awoke feeling refreshed. He lay in bed a moment longer, listening to birds chirping through the open window and the faint crackle of bacon sizzling in the kitchen. It was Sunday morning—he could tell without opening his eyes. The smell of breakfast, the sound of gospel choirs and fiery preachers on the AM radio atop the fridge, and the soft hum of his mother singing along—all of it wrapped him in a familiar warmth.

He sat up and watched the sunlight stream through the slats of the venetian blinds, illuminating dust particles dancing in the air. He knew he had to leave by 10:30 to make it back to the ship by evening. He gathered his toothbrush and razor and headed to the bathroom, where David was just stepping out.

"Hi, Pop," David said cheerfully. "Sleepyhead!"

"Hey, son. I guess I'm the last one," Tobias replied, rushing to get ready.

By the time he returned to the bedroom and dressed, his mother, sister, and son were already seated at the kitchen table. Tobias thought, *I could sure use one of those Jevmmunian valet consoles right now.*

"Come on, Pop!" David called out. "We're hungry!"

"I'm coming," Tobias said, smiling at the sound of family.

As he walked toward the kitchen, the doorbell rang.

"I'll get it," Tobias said.

He descended the stairs and looked through the peephole. It was Phillip.

Puzzled, Tobias opened the door. "Phillip? What are you doing here?"

"I'm here to stop you, Sinclair."

"Stop me from what? Mill isn't here. We're just friends."

"This isn't about Mill. I've come to stop *you*."

"What are you talking about?"

Phillip reached inside his jacket and pulled out a small black pistol. His face was stoic, his eyes cold. Tobias recognized the look—the same hollow expression he'd seen in the eyes of the crack addict who mugged him years ago. But Phillip wasn't desperate for a fix. He was deliberate. Calculated.

I'm not going to be a victim this time, Tobias thought. *I will not go down this way.*

He lunged forward, grabbing the gun and twisting Phillip's wrist. The two men struggled violently. The gun discharged, grazing Tobias's temple. Blood ran down his cheek. Phillip, shorter but stockier, used his weight to overpower Tobias, slamming him against the doorframe. Another shot rang out, shattering the glass pane.

David, hearing the commotion, ran downstairs. A third shot fired—striking David in the chest. He collapsed at the bottom of the stairs.

Janice screamed from the top of the staircase. "No!!!"

Fueled by adrenaline, Tobias twisted Phillip's wrist back until the gun discharged again—this time into Phillip's stomach. Phillip went limp. Tobias snatched the gun and threw it across the floor. Dizzy from his head wound, he staggered to David's side.

"David! David!" he cried, gently patting his son's face. "Sis, call 911!"

Janice ran to the nearest phone.

Tobias remembered the medallion around his neck. He pulled it out and pressed the button.

Stokes answered immediately. "Yes, Tobias?"

"I'm at home in Philadelphia," Tobias said, breathless. "A man tried to kill me. I was grazed, but he shot my son—and I shot him. I need help."

"Say no more."

Within thirty seconds, the spaceship hovered above the block. Tobias heard the commotion outside—screeching tires, panicked voices. The doorbell rang again, followed by a loud knock.

"Come in!" Tobias shouted.

Stokes entered, stepping over Phillip's body. "We must hurry. The ship is outside."

"I can't leave now!" Tobias cried. "My son may be dying!"

"We'll take them with us," Stokes said. "There's no time."

He dragged Phillip onto the porch. A crowd had gathered, staring at the lifeless body and the massive spacecraft above.

"Hurry, Tobias!" Stokes yelled. "Bring your son!"

Tobias carried David in his arms. Neighbors gasped. "He's dead!" someone cried. "Two of them are dead!"

As soon as Tobias stepped onto the porch, a beam of blue light shot from the underside of the ship, enveloping Tobias, David, Stokes, and Phillip. In less than three seconds, the light vanished—and so did they.

The crowd stared at the sky, watching a streak of white light disappear into the clouds while Janice remained on the phone with 911.

The four men materialized in the hub of the spacecraft, bathed in the glow of the blue light. Beatrice and Goren stood waiting near the central control panel. The two Naku pilots were already navigating the ship away from Philadelphia—away from Earth—and back toward the asteroid belt.

Within the beam, Tobias held his unconscious son. Stokes knelt beside Phillip, searching for a pulse that wasn't there. Goren turned a lever, dimming the blue light. With the ship now on a stable flight path, the Naku navigators joined Tobias and Stokes, guiding them down the corridor to the conference room—now transformed into a medical bay.

The conference table was gone. In its place stood two operating tables surrounded by surgical lasers, monitors, and glowing instruments. Tobias and Goren gently placed David on one table. Stokes and the Naku pilots lifted Phillip onto the other.

Tobias stepped back, unable to speak. He could only pray. Tears streamed down his face. Stokes placed a reassuring hand on his shoulder.

"Don't worry, Tobias," he said gently. "The Naku know what they're doing."

Stokes turned toward the door. "I need to monitor the autopilot." He left, leaving Tobias alone with Beatrice, who stood just outside the doorway.

She entered quietly, her eyes full of concern. "Tobias," she said softly. "Oh. You're hurt. Let me see."

She examined the gash near his temple, the blood drying on his cheek. "Sit down," she said, motioning to one of the chairs.

Tobias sat, eyes fixed on Goren as he worked on David—and on Phillip, whom Tobias now felt a deep aversion toward.

Beatrice retrieved a small bottle of antiseptic and a tube of salve from a hidden drawer. She cleaned the wound, then applied the salve. The gash closed almost instantly.

"You know," Tobias said, distracted, "I've never hated anyone in my life."

"I didn't hurt you that much, did I?" Beatrice asked, capping the salve.

Tobias smiled faintly. "Not you. Not at all. Thank you, Beatrice."

"Who do you hate?" she asked.

"That man on the table tried to kill me. He shot my son. He used to brutalize my best friend. If I should hate anyone, it should be him."

"Do you?"

Tobias paused. "Strangely, no. I don't really know him. Hatred is odd—it takes on a life of its own. I hate what he's done, but I don't hate him. With all my talk about forgiveness... I can't hate anyone anymore."

Beatrice nodded. "Such freedom."

"Yeah," Tobias said. "An odd kind of freedom."

He glanced at Goren. "So... Goren's a doctor too?"

"All Jevmmunians receive medical training," Beatrice explained. "The Naku take it especially seriously. After the Roswell crash in 1947, Goren requested extra training. He lost his best friend in that crash."

Tobias and Beatrice watched in silence. The Naku pilots shielded their thoughts, but Goren communicated telepathically: Both David and Phillip were dead when they arrived. We revived them. They will survive.

Goren turned to Tobias and offered a telepathic smile. Go to your quarters. We'll alert you when your son wakes up.

Beatrice stood and offered her hand. "Come, Tobias. I'll walk you back."

He took her hand and stood. As they walked down the corridor, Tobias kept glancing back at the conference room until the door slid shut.

"Your son is handsome," Beatrice said. "He takes after his father."

Tobias, still distracted, missed the compliment. He looked around the ship as if seeing it anew.

"How did you get us back so fast?" he asked. "What was that blue light?"

"In emergencies, we use the light instead of the ramp," Beatrice said. "Think of it like the transporter in Star Trek. We used it to bring Travis Walton aboard in 1975. His coworkers panicked and drove off. It was widely reported."

"That was *Fire in the Sky*, right?"

"Yes. It was true."

Tobias chuckled. "You and I always end up talking about movies."

"Only if I'm in them," Beatrice teased.

They both laughed. For a moment, Tobias felt lighter. He wasn't worried about David. He felt—for the first time—that his son was in good hands.

They stopped at his door.

"Get some rest, Tobias. You've been through a lot." She kissed him gently on the cheek and walked away.

Tobias watched her go, thinking how long it had been since he'd been touched with tenderness.

Tobias lay on his bed, eyes closed, mind racing. He couldn't sleep. He thought of David—how he would explain everything, how he would make sense of the impossible. He waited for Goren's update, but the silence gnawed at him.

Restless, Tobias activated the console in his quarters. Though the ship was nearly two hundred million miles from Earth, the console could receive transmissions—TV and radio signals traveling at light speed, arriving with a thirty-minute delay. He tuned into Philadelphia's local stations.

Janice's face filled the screen.

She was sobbing, still wearing her breakfast apron, collapsing into the arms of an EMS worker. Tobias's heart clenched. He switched channels, but every station showed the same footage: Janice, distraught, surrounded by reporters and crowds. An ambulance slowly pushed through the throngs. Another clip showed EMS workers wheeling his mother out of the house.

What have I done? Tobias thought, flipping through the coverage.

A reporter stood near the shattered front door of the Sinclair home. "Witnesses saw a beam of blue light emanate from the UFO," she said, pointing to the porch. "Tobias Sinclair, his son, and two other men allegedly vanished into thin air."

Cell phone videos played footage of the spacecraft hovering, the beam of light, the disappearance. Tobias watched his own vanishing, stunned. He scoured other networks—BBC, Canadian news, international feeds. The story was everywhere. His first contact program with Goren was being rebroadcast. Reporters ended segments with, "It was real."

The New School of Truth was under scrutiny. Mill and Jimmy were being questioned. Tobias saw reporters camped outside their homes. He tried calling Janice, Mill, Jimmy—no signal.

They finally believe me, he thought. But not like this.

He felt helpless. Guilty. He hadn't had time to prepare his loved ones. Mill knew about Jevmmuns, but not enough to answer questions. They were on their own.

Just then, Goren appeared at the door.

"Would you like to see your son, Tobias?"

Tobias stood, lightheaded. He'd lost track of time. The life he'd known was unraveling. He followed Goren down the corridor.

"David is sedated, but waking," said Goren. "It would comfort him to see your face first."

"How is he?"

"As you would say, 'good as new.' Earth's weapons are primitive but lethal. Fortunately, we've long mastered the repair of such wounds."

Goren spoke aloud but was telepathically aware of Tobias's anguish. "Don't worry about the disruption on Earth. We had no choice. You needed us. And we still need you."

"Thank you, Goren. For saving my son."

"We know you love him very much."

"I do."

They entered the conference room. David and Phillip lay on converted hospital beds, sleeping peacefully. The surgical assistants had returned to their duties.

"Now that you're here, we'll awaken David," said Goren. "Your presence will help him stay calm. He wasn't prepared to see Naku beings."

Tobias glanced at Phillip, sedated. "What will you do with him?"

"He tried to kill you. We'll keep him sedated until we learn more."

David stirred. His head moved side to side. He groaned.

Tobias took his hand and wiped his forehead with a cool cloth Goren had provided before quietly leaving the room.

"I'm here, son," Tobias whispered. "David, I'm here."

"No! I don't want to go back!" David cried, eyes still closed.

Tobias squeezed his hand gently.

"I want to stay here with you!" David said.

Tobias realized David wasn't speaking to him. Was he delirious? Dreaming? Somewhere else?

"What task do I need to finish?" David shouted. Then, eyes wide open: "Don't leave me!"

He looked around, startled by Phillip's presence. Then he saw Tobias—relieved, joyful, and frightened all at once.

"Pop! What happened? Where am I?"

"You're with me, son. Everything's going to be all right."

David paused, then smiled faintly. "I know," he said. "I was with Mom."

Tobias stared at his son, stunned. He wasn't prepared for what he'd just heard. The shock was written all over his face, though David didn't seem to notice.

"I was with Grandpa too," David said softly. "I didn't want to come back. It was peaceful there. Beautiful. Everyone was full of love."

Tobias could barely speak. "Do you mean… heaven?"

"I guess so, if that's what you want to call it," David replied. "All I know is, it was a place of joy and light. I think I must've been dead."

Tobias said nothing. There was nothing he could say.

David continued. "I didn't feel anything when I was shot. I remember lying at the bottom of the stairs, unable to move. Then I was floating—above the scene. I saw you fighting that man in the vestibule. I wanted to help, but I couldn't. I kept rising, out of the house, above the neighborhood. Then I saw a bright white light in the distance. It grew larger, brighter. It embraced me, Pop. I didn't want it to let me go."

Tobias took David's hand again, silently listening.

"Then I saw Grandpa," David said. "He looked just like I remembered. He didn't speak, but I could feel his love—it was radiant. He told me I was doing a good job helping Grandma, and that our family should stick together."

David paused, a tear sliding down his cheek. "Then Mom appeared. She was beautiful. Calm. Full of love. She told me to try to understand you. To give you a chance. She said it wasn't your fault that you left. She said you were chosen for a big task."

"A big task?" Tobias whispered.

"She said you're doing it now. And that it wasn't my time to stay in heaven. My task is to come back and help you. She told me not to be so sad all the time. That she's always with me."

Tobias smiled gently. Though his marriage to Sharon had faded long before her death, they'd never fought. They'd simply drifted apart. She'd focused on parenting; he'd focused on his career and later, his books. Now he wondered—had the extraterrestrials been guiding him even then? Had they nudged him toward this path?

David looked over at Phillip. "Isn't that the man you were fighting?"

Tobias nodded. "Yes."

David sat up, glancing around the sleek room. "Pop, what is this place? A hospital?"

"They used it as one," Tobias said gently. "The people here saved your life."

"What people?"

"We're on a spaceship, son."

"A spaceship?!"

"Don't be afraid. Remember my last program with Goren?"

"Yeah."

"Well, he saved your life."

David looked at Phillip. "Did he save his life too?"

"Yes."

David swung his legs over the edge of the bed. "Is everyone okay at home? Grandma? Aunt Janice?"

"As far as I know, yes. But it's a long story."

"What do you mean?"

"Everyone saw the spaceship take us away."

"This spaceship?! I guess I was unconscious."

"You were. But don't worry. You'll see it for yourself. It made news all over the world."

"I bet."

"In the meantime, I want you to get used to your surroundings. I'd like you to meet Goren and the others."

Tobias touched David's cheek. "You wouldn't be afraid to meet an alien up close, would you?"

David smiled. "If you put it that way, I guess not."

They talked quietly. Tobias filled David in on what to expect. No one interrupted. The crew gave them space. Tobias felt overwhelming gratitude. He hadn't lost his son. He'd been given a second chance.

Beatrice's voice came over the intercom, melodic and warm.

"Tobias, Goren would like to return to the conference room to check on his patients. Is that okay?"

Tobias looked at David, who nodded.

"Yes, Beatrice. It's okay. My son would like to meet his doctor. In fact, he'd like to meet everyone."

"I'll let Goren know."

Tobias turned to David. "They're being thoughtful about your visit. Remember, Goren looks just like he did on my program. And don't forget to thank him."

"Dad, I'm almost twenty-two. I've got this."

Moments later, the door slid open. Goren entered. David, sitting up, stared at him—fascinated, not afraid. Goren approached with a practiced smile and checked the monitors.

"How do you feel?" he asked.

"I feel fine," David replied. He glanced at Tobias, then back at Goren. "Thank you for saving my life."

"You're welcome, David. All life is precious. We hope you enjoy your time with us. We've prepared a room for you next to your father's."

"Just like old times," Tobias said.

He turned serious. "Thank you again, Goren. My son told me he had a near-death experience."

"That's not unusual," Goren said. "As we've become more skilled at saving lives, we've learned that the spirit persists. Many who were technically deceased report meeting loved ones in what you call heaven."

"I went through a bright white light," David said.

"That was your spirit transitioning," Goren replied. "You were adjusting to your pure energy state. All spirits in heaven travel at the speed of light."

As Goren continued examining David, he spoke calmly. "All beings are composed of matter and energy. Our bodies are matter. Our spirits—energy. When you died, David, your spirit connected with the energy of your loved ones. Their bodies had passed, but their spirits persisted. They became part of the white light, which contains all wavelengths of the spectrum. In that way, we are all eternal. We never truly die."

David was already growing fond of Goren. "Wow, Goren. That's deep."

Goren finished his examination and turned toward the sleeping Phillip. He craned his long neck over his shoulder. "On Jevmmuns, we don't have religions as you do on Earth. We use the New Science and objective observation to understand life and death. We don't fear death. We see it as part of the continuum."

He turned back to Phillip, leaving Tobias and David in quiet reflection.

"Come on," Tobias said gently. "Let's see your new room."

David stood easily, his body fully healed. They walked together toward the hub, where Tobias introduced him to the two Naku navigators. They nodded politely but remained aloof. David, unfazed, found them fascinating.

Stokes and Beatrice stood near the corridor entrance. Tobias approached with David close behind.

"David," Tobias said, "I'd like you to meet Beatrice and Stokes."

Beatrice extended her hand. "It's so nice to meet you, David."

David hesitated, then bowed slightly as he shook her hand. "Nice to meet you too."

Beatrice smiled. "I see David is as shy as his father."

Stokes winked at Tobias. "Don't mind her. Beatrice likes to tease newcomers. Welcome aboard, David."

"Thank you, sir," David replied.

"No need for 'sir.' Just Stokes will do."

Tobias chuckled. "Or maybe 'Fearless Leader'?"

They all laughed—until a loud explosion rocked the ship.

The spacecraft tilted sharply downward. All four were thrown to the floor. Tobias and David slid past the quarters, crashing into the far wall. Beatrice collided into Tobias. David grabbed a handle near the end of the corridor, stopping just short of impact.

The lights went out. A second explosion tilted the ship upward, slamming them against the adjacent wall.

In the hub, the Naku navigators worked feverishly to stabilize the ship, dodging an asteroid that had veered into their path. In the conference room, Goren had fallen but quickly strapped Phillip to the bed before using the intercom.

"Phillip and I are unharmed," he announced.

The corridor remained dark. Stokes called out, "Is everyone okay?"

Tobias, Beatrice, and David confirmed they weren't seriously injured.

"I thought we hit an asteroid," Stokes said. "But this is worse."

Suddenly, a booming voice echoed through the ship's address system.

"This is COL. Your activities have disrupted life on Earth. You must cease and desist!"

Stokes turned grim. "They're back."

The voice continued. "You have taken one of our Earth-based members. We want him back!"

The Naku stabilized the ship and restored the lights. Tobias, Stokes, Beatrice, and David rushed to the hub. Goren joined them.

Stokes shouted, "Can you hear us? We're trying to save lives!"

"You rejected our offer to work together," the voice replied. "You evaded us. You made first contact without our input. And now you've kidnapped one of our members!"

"We brought aboard two injured men," Stokes said. "We only wanted to save them."

"Nonsense!" Another explosion rocked the ship. The crew braced themselves.

"If you keep attacking us," Beatrice shouted, "you won't get your member back—or anything else!"

"So you admit he's a hostage!"

"I didn't say that," Beatrice replied. "Who is your member?"

A long pause. Then the voice returned.

"His name is Phillip Celdy. You interfered with his assignment. We demand his return!"

Tobias whispered to Stokes, "I guess Phillip's assignment was to kill me. He said he came to stop me."

Stokes spoke into the intercom. "Phillip was dead when we brought him aboard. He failed his mission."

"Is he still dead?"

"What was his assignment?"

"That is none of your concern. WE WANT HIM BACK!"

Suddenly, the Naku navigators accelerated the ship at lightning speed toward Mars. The COL ship fired one last shot—missing by far. Unable to track the Council's evasive maneuvers, the COL vessel fell behind.

They were safe. For now.

Tobias turned to Goren. "Do you think they're following us?"

Goren replied both verbally and telepathically, for David's sake. "No. They'll return to Earth and wait for us there. We underestimated how quickly they'd come back to this solar system."

Stokes added, "I'm glad we made our presence known when we did. With COL snooping around, our mission just got harder."

Beatrice turned to Tobias. "How much do you know about Phillip? COL seemed desperate to get him back."

"Not much," Tobias said. "He was the abusive ex-husband of my closest friend. I didn't even know he was connected to COL."

112

"It's time to awaken him," Goren said, heading toward the conference room. "Would you like to come, Tobias? He's already secured."

"Yes," Tobias replied. He turned to his son. "David, could you wait here?"

David hesitated. "Sure, Pop. Though I'd like to hear what he has to say."

Goren looked at David. "You may come, if you wish. You have a right to see the man who nearly killed you."

Tobias nodded. David followed them into the conference room. Stokes and Beatrice remained at the hub, assisting the Naku navigators as they kept the ship in evasive orbit behind Mars, hidden from COL's sensors.

Inside the conference room, Goren administered a drug to awaken Phillip.

"Shouldn't you leave the room?" Tobias asked. "Has he been prepped to see you—or the ship?"

"If he's with COL," Goren replied, "he already knows about us."

Phillip's chest began to heave. His peaceful expression twisted into a grimace. He opened his eyes and locked onto Goren, showing no surprise at the sight of a Naku. Then he turned and saw Tobias and David.

"You!" Phillip shouted. "You're alive, Sinclair?"

"So are you," Tobias said calmly.

Phillip struggled against his restraints. "Let me go! Where am I?"

"You're aboard a spacecraft," Goren answered. "Your friends from COL are asking for your safe return."

Phillip laughed bitterly. "They may have asked for it—but it wouldn't be so safe."

Goren, reading Phillip's mind, sensed no immediate threat. He loosened the restraints.

Tobias stepped forward, voice rising. "Goren, do you know what you're doing? This man tried to kill me!" David held his father back by grabbing his arm.

"Sinclair," Phillip said, "you don't have to worry about me anymore. I'm safe now."

Tobias snapped, *"You're* safe? What about *us?*"

Phillip looked at David. "I'm sorry I tried to kill you, Sinclair. And I'm sorry you were hurt, young man."

"My name is David."

"I'm sorry, David," Phillip said. "I see things differently now. I'm not the same man."

Tobias grimaced. "Not the same as what?"

Phillip stared ahead. "After I was shot, I found myself in a place of turmoil. It was stuffy, humid, crimson. Unseen hands grabbed at me. I felt everything I'd ever done wrong. I felt Mill's pain—every moment of it. I was alone. I knew I deserved it."

Goren looked at Tobias and David and telepathically assured them: He's sincere.

Then, aloud, Goren said, "Most who return from death report experiences shaped by their behavior in life. You'd call it karma."

114

Phillip nodded. "I thought I'd be tortured forever. Then you brought me back. Thank you."

Tobias calmed. David released his arm.

Tobias stepped closer. "Why did you try to kill me?"

"COL recruited me," Phillip said. "They told me they'd kill me if I didn't kill you."

"They despised me that much?"

"They despised what you were doing. You were undermining their control over first contact."

"Why you?"

"They knew you were close to Mill. They used me to get to you."

"You used Mill to get to me?"

Phillip looked down. "It was wrong. I know that now. After what I experienced… I seek sanctuary. If I go back to COL, they'll kill me."

Tobias turned to Goren. "What is all this talk of killing? I thought Jevmmuns was a planet of peace."

Goren replied, "COL is a renegade group. They reject the New Science. They use violence to achieve their goals. They are a menace."

Phillip stood facing Tobias, David behind him. His expression was serene—unlike anything Tobias had seen before. Goren gave a reassuring smile, confirming Phillip's sincerity.

Phillip extended his hand to Tobias. "Sinclair," he said, "I also learned in that other world, in the afterlife, that forgiveness is the key to life. Will you please forgive me?"

Tobias looked at Phillip's outstretched hand, then into his eyes. In that moment, he saw not just a man seeking redemption, but the culmination of everything he had ever taught. His books, his lectures, his Day of Forgiveness campaign—all of it pointed to this one decision. If he couldn't forgive Phillip now, it would all be hypocrisy.

He glanced at David, watching silently nearby. Tobias knew this was his chance to model something deeper than strength—it was his chance to show his son what it meant to be a man of integrity. He took Phillip's hand and pulled him into a warm embrace. "I forgive you, man," Tobias said, patting Phillip's back.

David and Goren looked on.

Phillip then turned to David and offered his hand. David hesitated. He could still see the fight, the gun, the fear. He looked down, trying to hide the storm inside him.

"I understand that it may be hard to forgive the man who nearly took your life," Phillip said gently. "But I just want you to know I'm sorry—from the bottom of my heart. If I could change what happened, I would. Let's be grateful we both have a second chance."

David looked up and glared. "Or a second chance to finish what you started," he muttered, then turned and walked out into the corridor.

Phillip stood with his hand still outstretched, visibly shaken. Tobias stepped beside him. "He's young. He'll understand in time."

Phillip nodded. "Mill and I never had children. But I think I can understand what this must be like for David."

Tobias found David pacing in the corridor. David stopped when he saw his father and stared at him, eyes burning.

"How could you hug that man?! For all intents and purposes, he killed me!"

"You're not dead now, are you?"

"No thanks to him. You always choose others before me. You always place me last!"

"David," Tobias said calmly, "haven't you learned anything from your near-death experience?"

David stood silently, shoulders trembling. Tobias placed a hand on his son's shoulder.

"To forgive him—or to forgive me—isn't really for him or me. It's for you. I'm trying to put *you* first, not last. I want you to be free, too."

"Free from what?" David asked, his voice softening.

"Free from anger, bitterness, and hate. The only way to do that is to forgive, son. You said you'd been to a beautiful place of love and forgiveness. Where is it now?"

David looked at his father. "It's always here."

Tobias nodded. "Then act like it, my son. Act like it. That place isn't just in heaven—it can be here on Earth, too. You decide."

David's eyes welled up. Tobias put his arm around him. "Come on. Let's see what your room looks like."

Tobias left David's quarters to give him space to settle in. But he returned a little while later with a surprise: a Jevmmunian version of a guitar, borrowed from Stokes. The instrument had a sleek, silvery body and strings that shimmered faintly in the light.

David's eyes lit up. He cradled the guitar like a long-lost friend, strumming softly, testing its tone. Then he looked up at Tobias, stunned.

"You got this for me?"

"I figured you might want something familiar," Tobias said. "Something that feels like home."

David hugged him—warmly, tightly. It felt like the first real embrace they'd shared in years.

"Pop… this means a lot. You really do care."

Tobias smiled, his voice quiet. "I told you I'd try for you, my son."

He watched David strum a gentle melody, his posture relaxed, his face softened. It was the first time since Tobias had returned that he'd seen his son smile with genuine joy—free from bitterness, free from pain.

Tobias thought, *I guess Stokes won't be seeing his guitar anytime soon.*

He sat beside David and said, "Maybe you could write some new songs while you're here."

David nodded. "I think I will."

Tobias looked at him, heart full. "I used to say forgiveness was liberation. But I never knew how much I needed it until now."

David paused, then smiled again—this time with understanding.

Chapter 8

Collision Course

As Tobias prepared for Wednesday's broadcast, he remembered Yolanda's suggestion: let Earth hear from a human face of Jevmmuns. He found Beatrice in the conference room, sipping her mint tea.

"Beatrice," he said, "would you consider appearing on the program? I think Earth needs to hear from someone like you."

She smiled warmly. "I'd be honored, Tobias. It's time they knew the truth. We broke all protocols by using the ship to rescue you in Philadelphia," Beatrice said. "The Council won't be pleased when they learn how we made first contact. But Earth is paying attention now."

Tobias smiled. "That's quite an understatement, Beatrice."

She nodded. "Bringing the ship to Philadelphia disrupted the global economy, triggered political unrest, and shook the mental stability of the human race. You've only seen snippets on your console, Tobias. We've been monitoring global communications. Fear is spreading. Many believe this is the end."

Beatrice glanced at her screen. "I was just reviewing the Jevmmunian crisis from centuries ago—how they managed public panic when the Naku returned."

"But that situation was different," Tobias said. "The people of Jevmmuns knew they came from elsewhere. They had legends about the Naku. Earthlings think they're alone in the universe."

"Not anymore," Beatrice replied. "Now they want answers."

"Then let's give them some," Tobias said. "You're the best person for the job."

"Why me?"

"Logic," Tobias said. "I'm not from Jevmmuns. Goren and the Naku weren't present during the enlightenment period. You were. You're the historian. The anthropologist. You understand the arc."

Beatrice finished her tea. "You make a convincing case."

Tobias leaned forward, energized. "We're going to host an interview to top all interviews. We'll calm their fears. Offer a new path. Call it our 'second first contact.' We'll help save Earth."

Over the next day, Tobias and Beatrice immersed themselves in Jevmmunian and Earth history. They rehearsed tone, phrasing, and key messages, hoping to ease the growing anxiety reflected across Earth's media. Humanity had questions—but no enemy to blame. The threat was internal: fear, ignorance, and the limits of imagination. Tobias and Beatrice were determined to change that.

The rest of Tuesday felt surreal. The ship maintained a wide elliptical orbit around Mars, evasive and unsettling. Tobias and Beatrice worked tirelessly. David stayed in his quarters, strumming his guitar, composing a song about his recent journey. Goren and the navigators focused on evading COL and boosting the signal. Stokes kept close to Phillip, probing for intel. Each crew member had a role. With clarity came a fragile calm. Tobias sensed it: the quiet before the storm.

Wednesday began smoothly. The ship remained hidden from COL. Goren secured the broadcast signal. Stokes monitored Phillip. David stayed close to his guitar. Most importantly, Tobias and Beatrice felt ready.

Tobias stepped away to visit David.

He knocked. "David?"

David opened the door. "Not interrupting, Pop. Just working on a song."

"You ready for the program?"

"As ready as I'll ever be," Tobias said. "I'm interviewing Beatrice. Goren's appearance last time was too much for people to digest."

"Or believe," David said. "But after seeing us take off in a flying saucer? Yeah, they believe something now."

"We're trying to calm them. Explain our intentions."

David chuckled. "You've got me, Pop. What *are* you trying to do?"

Tobias smiled. "We want to show there's nothing to fear. Jevmmuns offers a roadmap—an example of how to avoid the pitfalls we're facing."

"You mean they want to be a role model?"

"Not exactly. They're offering information. Tools. They've seen Earth destroy itself before. They want to help us avoid doing it again."

"But how can they help when COL wants to kill us?"

"They're nonviolent. I don't think COL wants to destroy the Council—just me."

"You? Why?"

"Because first contact is happening through my program. Through the New Science I've taught."

David's eyes widened. "Whoever controls you, controls first contact."

"Exactly. That's why I've chosen to stay with the Council."

Tobias paused. "Listen, I wanted to ask—would you appear on the show with me? Your aunt and grandmother need to see you're alive and well."

"Sure, Pop. What do I need to say?"

"Whatever you want. Or just flash that goofy smile of yours," Tobias said, poking David playfully.

David grinned. "Okay. I'll show my face."

"Good. Meet me in the conference room when you're ready."

Tobias returned to his quarters, deliberately avoiding the media screen. He didn't want Earth's chaos clouding his focus. He thought of Mill's advice—meditation, yoga. He calmed his mind, refreshed himself with a waterless cleansing, and changed into another silver spacesuit. *Shiny, comfortable pajamas,* he mused, clearing his thoughts for the broadcast.

As the time approached, Tobias walked to the ship's hub. Goren looked up from the controls and approached.

"Tobias," Goren said, both telepathically and aloud, "I wish you success. I understand your choice to use a human face for this introduction."

"I'm glad you understand," Tobias replied. "We may have pushed too hard last time. But soon, humans will be ready to see Naku faces every day."

"I hope they'll see us as friendly beings," Goren said. "Humans tend to operate from fear. Tobias, I can tell you now—this week's program is being highly anticipated. The media, governments, and the general population are all watching. No one has blocked our access to the Internet or satellite systems. For two days, the only content available has been footage of our ship and rebroadcasts of last week's program. The world is waiting."

"Well, I'm sure glad I don't have stage fright," Tobias quipped, masking his rising anxiety.

122

He glanced around the hub. "Where's Stokes?"

"He's keeping our guest occupied," Goren replied. Then, telepathically: We haven't told Phillip about today's broadcast. If he's still working with COL, we risk sabotage. Stokes will keep him distracted.

Tobias nodded. "That's what I call great teamwork."

Goren turned back to the controls. "Don't worry. The signal will be strong and clear. And I believe your message will be, too."

"It will be," Tobias said, heading down the corridor.

Beatrice and David were already waiting at the conference room door, chatting like old friends. Tobias approached, smiling.

"Ready to make some history?" he asked.

They both smiled back, bolstered by Tobias's quiet confidence.

Inside, Tobias and Beatrice sat at the center of the table. David sat off to the side, unsure of what he'd say. The lights dimmed. Hidden cameras activated. Tobias, now a seasoned host, spoke naturally to his unseen audience.

"Hello everyone. This is Tobias Sinclair, and welcome to the New School of Truth. We're broadcasting from an undisclosed location. I want to calm any fears about the spacecraft you saw in Philadelphia. No one was abducted. We were rescued. The ill among us received life-saving treatment. This is my son, David. His life was saved by the people aboard this ship. I'll be forever grateful."

The camera cut to David, who gave a subtle smile and waved.

Tobias nodded, encouraging him to speak.

"Hello," David said, voice soft. "This is all new to me—just like it is to you. I've seen the videos. I'm still shocked."

He paused, looked down, then at his father. Tobias smiled, silently urging him on.

"I just want to say I'm okay. I especially want my grandmother and aunt to know—we're okay. Don't worry. The people on this ship healed me. I'm back to normal."

David's voice grew stronger.

"And I want to give a shout-out to the Olive Branch Nursing Home. Stay calm. Stay strong. I'll be back to sing more songs soon."

He paused, taking in the moment.

"I've seen a lot these past few days. All I can say is—we shouldn't be afraid. Young people like me need to know we have a future. My father's New Science makes sense to me. And I'm not saying that just because I'm his son. Our eyes are just beginning to open. That's all I can say."

Tobias smiled. "Thank you, David. You make me proud."

David looked relieved. He'd said what he needed to say—and now he could simply watch.

Tobias turned back to the camera.

"Many of you have studied last week's program. The events in Philadelphia changed how people view that broadcast. Many now believe it was real. I'm glad you believe Goren is a member of an intelligent species called the Naku—descendants of Earth's dinosaurs. He lives on Jevmmuns, a planet where humans and Naku coexist."

Tobias looked at Beatrice and smiled.

"Today, I have another guest from Jevmmuns. She's a human whose ancestors left Earth tens of thousands of years ago. Her planet once faced the same turmoil we face now—political division, religious conflict, racism, war, pollution. But they found a way forward. Please welcome Beatrice of Jevmmuns."

"Thank you, Tobias," she said warmly.

"Beatrice, you're an anthropologist and historian. What parallels do you see between Earth and Jevmmuns?"

"Our planet was much like yours," she said, speaking gently to the camera. "We had countries, wealth and poverty, and electronic sophistication. But our technology magnified our disparities. Those at the bottom could see how the top lived. We saw how we treated one another—and it forced us to change."

Tobias nodded. "On Earth, cell phone cameras have exposed police killings of unarmed African Americans. Those videos have united people globally to confront racism and bigotry."

"Yes," Beatrice said. "That's how we began to change. Our first step was awareness. Then came action."

She paused.

"Our most prominent social pioneer, Greta Stokes, once asked: Is that all you can see? A color? A nationality? A religion? An ethnicity? Do you not see the human being? The answer was always more complicated than the question."

She turned to Tobias. "Tell me—what has Earth done with its new awareness?"

Tobias sighed. "Not much, I'm ashamed to say."

"On Jevmmuns, once we saw our mistakes, we set out to change."

125

"Sounds hard," Tobias said. "How did you do it?"

Beatrice's voice was calm, but resolute.

"We opened a dialogue between all people. When disagreements arose, we examined the root causes. We realized that every society was shaped by ancestors long gone—and that we were reacting to consequences they left behind. But those ancestors are no longer here. We are. And we have the power to choose what to carry forward."

She paused, letting the weight of her words settle.

"We chose to perpetuate the good and eliminate the bad. We continued our scientific and technological progress but rejected the social biases and bigotry that had been passed down. As Greta Stokes once said: 'The ancestors have merged with the universe. Let us use the legacy of their good, and reject the prejudices they developed to reach this point. Let us only use the cream off the top—the best of the best—to build our society. Then we will all become the crème de la crème.'"

The camera cut briefly to Tobias and David, both smiling—expressions of hope and inspiration.

"That sounds great," Tobias said. "But was it really possible to do that systematically?"

"Yes," Beatrice replied. "Every event has a cause and an effect. We learned to challenge the cause to improve the effect—and eliminate the problem."

"Can you give us an example?"

"Certainly. You mentioned Earth's mistreatment of people of color. On Jevmmuns, we had similar issues. But we stopped thinking of race as a concept. We recognized that physical differences are simply environmental adaptations— nothing more. Judging people by appearance is behavior fit for lower animals. We are spirits in human bodies. The body is temporary. The spirit is eternal."

Tobias was captivated—not just by her words, but by her presence.

"I visited Jevmmuns," he said. "I saw your peaceful, inclusive society. Earth could learn so much. Could you tell us how your society is governed?"

"Well…"

Suddenly, a deafening explosion rocked the ship. The lights went out. The walls shook. The spacecraft twisted violently, nearly flipping upside down. Monitoring screens went dark. David was thrown across the table, smashing the teapot and sending cups flying. Beatrice hit the floor. Tobias clung to a swivel chair as it skidded across the room.

Then came the voice.

"This is COL. How foolish you were to broadcast to Earth! Your signal made it easy to find you. The broadcast is now terminated. Surrender or be destroyed. We want Tobias Sinclair and Phillip Celdy. Now!"

The Naku navigators scrambled to stabilize the ship. Lights flickered back on. Smoke billowed from the control panel. Tobias helped Beatrice to her feet. David lay near the head of the table, clutching his wrist.

"David!" Tobias called. "Are you alright?"

"I think I broke my wrist," David groaned.

Tobias helped him up. Beatrice opened the door and they rushed to the hub. Goren and Stokes were assisting the crew. Phillip stood silently near the corridor entrance, watching.

"Goren!" Tobias shouted. "David's hurt!"

Goren hurried over. "I need to examine him in the conference room," he said telepathically. He and David left.

Beatrice joined the crew at the control panel. Stokes took over Goren's duties. Phillip approached Tobias.

"What was this broadcast? What signal did COL detect?"

"It was my program," Tobias said. "Cable and Internet. Until we were rudely interrupted."

"No one told me," Phillip said. "I guess I'm not as trusted here as I thought. But I could've warned you—COL can detect any electromagnetic transmission. They were waiting."

The voice returned.

"Our patience is growing thin. Send Sinclair and Celdy in the blue beam of light."

Stokes replied, "You damaged our ship. The beam system is offline. We need time to repair."

"Then land on Mars," COL commanded.

"We cannot," Stokes replied. "You damaged our life support unit in that last attack. We need to return to Earth for repairs. Otherwise, we'll all die."

The voice from COL grew harsher. "You speak as if we care about your lives! We intend to execute Celdy and Sinclair. We will not hesitate to kill you as well!"

Stokes stood firm. "Are we not a people of peace? Do you want our blood on your hands?"

A pause. Then the voice relented. "Very well. You cannot land on Mars due to atmospheric conditions. We will allow you to return to Earth for repairs. Celdy and Sinclair may then come to our ship. We will escort you to your preferred location in upstate New York."

Beatrice leaned toward Stokes and whispered, "They know more about us than we know about them."

The damaged ship limped away from Mars, COL's vessel trailing close behind. The journey to Earth took over seven minutes—agonizingly slow. As they entered orbit, the mood aboard the Council's ship was somber. COL had disrupted their broadcast, undermined their mission, and asserted dominance. The crew felt defeated. Tobias and Phillip felt like bargaining chips—trapped rats on a sinking ship.

Yet Tobias couldn't shake a question.

"Isn't it strange?" he asked Phillip. "They announced their plan to execute us. Why not just destroy the ship?"

Phillip nodded. "Stokes may be right. COL might need the Council. Or they need you—for something."

"They want to use me," Tobias said. "Make me their symbolic leader. Control first contact. Claim legitimacy."

Phillip agreed. "That was their plan. When I failed to eliminate you, they punished me. But they still want you."

Tobias smirked bitterly. "Like a jealous spouse—if they can't have me, no one can."

Phillip looked serious. "They avoided destroying the ship. They still need you."

Tobias clenched his jaw. "I won't be used anymore. I've had enough."

The voice returned, slightly less harsh. "We are now in Earth's orbit. We will wait until nightfall to land."

Tobias excused himself and walked the corridor, trying to calm his fury. He headed to the conference room to check on David. He trusted Goren—species didn't matter. What mattered was integrity.

The door slid open. David sat on the table, now an examining bed. Goren hovered nearby, holding a device that resembled a microphone.

"You've come at the right time," Goren said. "I'm all done."

Tobias smiled at his son. "Hi, Pop," David said, flexing his wrist and fingers. "Feels like it never happened."

Tobias turned to Goren. "You're quite a physician. Thank you."

Goren nodded. "We all train in the healing arts. But the real credit goes to the technology." He held up the device. "It accelerates bone knitting exponentially."

David grinned. "Well, thanks to both of you."

Goren smiled—his lips more natural now, clearly practicing for his human friends. He left the room. Tobias and David walked together to David's quarters.

"I hope Goren doesn't send us a medical bill," Tobias joked. "We couldn't afford it."

David chuckled, picking up his guitar and strumming it softly. "I hope Grandma and Aunt Janice got the message. I hope they're okay. Why did COL attack us?"

Tobias sighed. "Same reason most people attack—power and control. One group trying to prove they're better than another."

"Even in outer space," David said.

"We're in Earth's orbit now," Tobias told him. "Waiting for nightfall to land in upstate New York."

"Upstate New York?" David laughed. "I thought it'd be Area 51!"

Tobias smiled. "Don't laugh too hard. These guys were involved in Roswell, too."

David grew serious. "Pop, how did you get mixed up in all this?"

"They chose me. Tried to influence my mind telepathically. After the mugging and seizures, something went wrong. People from Jevmmuns contacted me. Eventually, they cured me. But the damage was done. They said Earth wasn't ready for the New Science."

"And that's why you left?"

"I had to. COL wanted to kidnap or kill me. I had to leave Earth for protection."

Tobias looked at David. "Right now, COL wants me and Phillip."

David stared, bracing for another goodbye. He set down his guitar.

"David," Tobias said gently, "we're heading into unknown territory. I may be forced to go with COL. But no matter what happens, I love you. I'm your father."

"You can't go," David said. "They want to kill you!"

"If I don't, they'll kill all of us."

"Then I'll go with you."

"No," Tobias said firmly. "You need to stay. Help Grandma and Aunt Janice. Keep the family together. Work with Jimmy and Mill if you want to help with my school and programs."

Tobias placed a hand on David's arm.

"You are my legacy—more than any book or lecture. You are my son."

"But Pop…" Tobias raised a finger to his lips. David fell silent. In that moment, they both understood—it had to be this way.

A heavy silence settled between them, broken only by quiet tears as they embraced. The possibility of parting—perhaps permanently—hung in the air like a storm cloud.

They remained in David's quarters, saying nothing. David sat on his bed, gently strumming his guitar, rocking back and forth. Tobias sat at the desk, lost in thought, meditating as he listened to the calming music.

Nightfall arrived in the Western Hemisphere. It was time to leave orbit.

Darkness blanketed North America. From space, the cities glowed faintly—sequins on a dark dress. Even the largest metropolises seemed subdued, their rhythms slowed by the natural cycles of Earth. In the quiet, nocturnal creatures stirred. And so did COL.

They, too, needed the cover of night to set their plans in motion. Yet, their plans needed more than the night to clothe the nakedness of their misguided strategy.

Tobias had drifted off in David's chair. David was still composing when the familiar voice echoed through the ship's address system.

"It is time to leave orbit and head for the landing area!"

Tobias stirred awake. David set down his guitar.

132

"Let's go to the hub," Tobias said, voice hoarse. "I want you to see the observation window."

"Okay, Pop."

They walked together to the hub. The crew was already assembled. Goren and the Naku navigators worked
the controls. Stokes, Beatrice, and Phillip stood at the observation window.

Tobias and David joined them. The ship was descending. The curvature of Earth's dark hemisphere loomed below. COL's ship trailed behind, distant but precise.

From this angle, Earth looked somber—its lit cities scattered like embers. The sunlit side was barely visible, leaving the planet to resemble a new moon.

They descended toward the northeastern United States. The night was clear. City lights traced a glowing chain from Washington, D.C. to Boston.

Phillip stood off to the side. Tobias and David stood between Stokes and Beatrice.

"Ever seen anything like this, David?" Stokes asked.

"No," David whispered. "Never."

Stokes leaned toward Tobias. "Goren has a plan."

Tobias glanced at him, but Stokes kept his eyes on the window.

The ship flew up the East Coast, past Washington and Baltimore. Suddenly, COL's voice blared through the address system.

"Why are you taking this route? There is much human activity here! Approach from the north and west!"

No one responded. The ship continued past Philadelphia, heading toward New York City.

"Stop!" the voice shouted. "Stop!"

Then—an explosion.

The ship lurched forward, spinning violently. It passed Staten Island and the Verrazano-Narrows Bridge, flying low over One World Trade Center and the skyscrapers of lower Manhattan.

A second blast missed, lighting up the East River near the Williamsburg Bridge.

The five humans at the window clung to the railing and to each other. The ship spun at a right angle. Goren and the navigators fought to stabilize it.

Then—one final blast.

It struck.

The ship split in two.

The larger section tumbled above the FDR Drive and crashed onto First Avenue, engulfed in flames in front of the United Nations building.

The smaller piece smashed into the sea wall and sank into the East River.

COL's ship hovered briefly above the wreckage, assessing the damage. Then, in a streak of white light, it vanished.

The dirty deed was done.

Chapter 9

Cautiously Optimistic

Fire trucks and police cars arrived almost immediately, cordoning off the wreckage and extinguishing the flames. Tobias and Beatrice still clung to the railing—now exposed to open air and the asphalt of First Avenue. The observation window was gone, replaced by smoke and chaos.

Stokes lay unconscious near the control panel, while Goren struggled to his feet. David had been thrown near the corridor entrance, along with one of the Naku navigators, who remained unconscious. One-third of the spacecraft—containing the conference room corridor—was missing. Phillip and the other navigator had been in that section. Both had drowned before rescue was possible.

The survivors were rushed to New York University Hospital in separate ambulances. There was no secrecy, no cover-up. Thanks to Tobias's first contact programs and the Philadelphia rescue, the public already knew. Strangely, no panic followed. In that way, first contact was a success.

Authorities interviewed each survivor about the attack and their knowledge of Jevmmuns and the Naku. The public, far from shocked, seemed relieved—finally, the truth was out.

Esmos, the surviving Naku navigator, was the most seriously injured. Goren, though recovering himself, advised the doctors. Remembering that the Naku evolved from Earth's dinosaurs and shared traits with birds, Goren recommended consulting a veterinarian specializing in avian care. The suggestion worked. Esmos underwent surgery and made a full recovery.

Tobias, David, Esmos, Goren, Stokes, and Beatrice were placed in a secure hospital unit. The Jevmmunian spacecraft had protected them during the crash—

its sonic sensors had suspended their bodies to minimize trauma. Injuries were mostly minor: abrasions, contusions, and smoke inhalation.

Each survivor was medically cleared and given a private room. They could visit one another freely. Even Esmos, once aloof, began to engage. Government officials conducted confidential interviews, but only Tobias and David had family on Earth. They were the only ones who received visitors.

Rebecca and Janice had been in protective custody since the Philadelphia incident. Escorted by three agents, they arrived at the hospital a week later. Rebecca, in a flowered dress, sat in a wheelchair pushed by one agent. Janice walked behind her, flanked by the others.

David spotted them first and rushed down the corridor, followed by Tobias. The family embraced in tears.

"Oh David!" Janice sobbed. "When you were shot and I couldn't help you, I thought we'd lost you. When we saw you on your father's program last week, we screamed with joy!"

Rebecca, still seated, held Tobias's hand. "The Lord spared you. You're still with us. That's a blessing."

Tobias, overwhelmed, said, "I didn't mean to put you through this. I didn't know any of this would happen."

Rebecca and Janice were given rooms on the unit. They didn't care that they couldn't return home—their neighborhood had become a tourist attraction. The family was together again. That was enough.

The unit began to feel like home. Tobias and Janice resumed their daily brother-sister talks. Rebecca watched the home shopping channel. David played his guitar. The rhythm of life returned, however altered.

Stokes, Beatrice, Goren, and Esmos were interviewed daily. They cooperated fully but avoided mentioning the Council's earthbound operatives— the ones who had delivered the cars to upstate New York. The vehicles were impounded but untraceable. The government suspected both COL and the Council still had help on Earth.

Jimmy and Mill visited regularly, traveling from Brooklyn by subway. Their arrival always felt like old times. Together, they brainstormed next steps for the New School of Truth and Tobias's Internet program. Each visit was a spark—a reminder that the mission wasn't over.

"How are they treating you, T.S.?" Jimmy asked during a visit.

Tobias chuckled. "That sounds like something you'd ask a prisoner on death row. Honestly, I don't feel like I'm being held against my will. I get why they're keeping us here, but I don't think they know what to do with us—especially Goren and Esmos."

Jimmy nodded. "They can't cover it up now. Everyone saw the spacecraft. No more weather balloon excuses."

"No, not this time," Tobias said, shaking his head. "That story died with Roswell. The truth's out. I introduced the world to Goren. We've already told them about Jevmmuns. Openness saved us."

"Otherwise," Mill added, "they'd have buried the whole thing."

Jimmy leaned forward. "So what's next?"

Tobias paused. "I don't believe in coincidences. We crashed in front of the United Nations. Maybe fate's telling us to go back—to share what we know with the world."

Jimmy grinned. "Makes sense. All nations should be involved."

"Exactly," Tobias said. "From the beginning, the idea was to see ourselves as one species. Nations are secondary."

"Being human is more important than being American or Nigerian or Japanese," Jimmy said. "Maybe we should rename it the United Species of One."

Mill, mostly quiet until now, raised an eyebrow. "Have you been watching TV lately?"

"No, why?"

"Well, don't let it go to your head, but people are calling you a hero."

"A hero?"

"Yes," she said, rolling her eyes. "They say your programs ushered in a new way of thinking. You've made the world aware of our true history—and of Jevmmuns and the Naku. Some folks online think you're a mythical figure."

"Oh no, not again."

"Again?" Jimmy asked.

"COL put me on a pedestal once. They wanted to kidnap me. That kind of thinking started this whole mess. I'm no hero."

Mill smiled. "You are to us."

Tobias shook his head. "False adulation doesn't help. The ship's destroyed. No one's going back to Jevmmuns. Goren, Esmos, Beatrice, and Stokes are stranded. Eventually, we'll die out. The records will be lost. Humanity will forget—just like Atlantis and Lemuria. Tobias Sinclair will fade into legend, if that."

Mill smirked. "Welcome to the club. You've finally become as pessimistic as I am."

They laughed.

"Unless…"

"Unless what?"

"Unless COL comes back."

Jimmy frowned. "Why would they?"

"Better question: why haven't they? They brushed the Council aside. Shouldn't they be initiating first contact?"

"They did more than brush them aside, T.S. They blew you out of the sky."

"Exactly. But where are they now? To the victor go the spoils, right?"

Mill nodded. "Earth hasn't heard from them since the attack. Maybe they returned to Jevmmuns."

"I doubt it. If they did, they'd know months would pass here before they could return. My guess? They're taking their time."

"Ask Stokes or Beatrice," Mill suggested. "They know COL better than we do."

"Good idea," Tobias said. "We always end up brainstorming when we're together."

Unbeknownst to Tobias, governments worldwide were already mobilizing. The attack had been witnessed by millions. Fear spread that Earth might be next.

Investigators recovered both pieces of the wreckage. They began reverse-engineering the technology, enlisting Goren and Esmos to help. The bodies of Phillip and the other Naku navigator were found in the East River.

Mill, as Phillip's ex-wife and next of kin, was asked about the remains.

"I guess they had to come to me," she told Tobias. "Otherwise, it would've been Potter's Field. He never treated me well, but I couldn't let him be buried like he had no one."

Tobias hesitated. "Sounds like you forgave him."

Mill looked down, silent.

Tobias didn't have the heart to tell her the full truth—that Phillip had only reentered her life to get closer to Tobias, that he was COL's assassin. But he sensed Mill already knew.

"I didn't know him well," Tobias said.

"You didn't miss much."

"He wanted us to believe he was innocent. That we could trust him."

"He could be charming," Mill said. "But with Phillip, you had to keep your guard up."

Tobias nodded. "Hard to warm up to someone who tried to kill me and my son." He paused. "So… are you going to have a funeral?"

"No," Mill said. "I'm going to have him cremated and scatter his ashes to the wind."

"To the wind?"

"Yes. That way, I'll know he can never hurt me again."

Tobias nodded. "Sounds like you're doing this more for yourself than for him."

Mill's voice softened. "Well, Toby, it's about time he gave something back to me. I finally deserve it."

They talked late into the evening. One unexpected gift of Tobias's five-month absence was the bond that had formed between Jimmy, Mill, and Tobias's family. David and Jimmy, close in age, had become fast friends. And now, Tobias was able to introduce his loved ones to the four Jevmmunians on the unit. Despite initial apprehension, the meetings went smoothly.

The hospital staff and government officials encouraged Tobias to resume his Internet and cable program. They believed the public deserved to hear directly from him. His show would now air across radio, television, and online platforms. Transparency was key—they wanted to avoid conspiracy theories and misinformation.

Tobias couldn't shake the feeling that the crash in front of the United Nations was no accident. During one of his interviews with government officials, he asked to address the UN. Days later, permission was granted. He would relaunch his program with a global broadcast from the UN General Assembly.

Weeks later, Tobias was escorted by police motorcade from the hospital to the UN. With him were Goren, Beatrice, Stokes, and Esmos. David came for moral support. Rebecca and Janice watched from the hospital. Mill and Jimmy tuned in from Brooklyn.

Inside the General Assembly, delegates from every nation filled the auditorium. Many wore headphones, listening to interpreters. Tobias stepped to the podium. Behind him sat the four Jevmmunians. David stood just out of frame.

After a long pause, Tobias began in a low, humble voice.

"Honored delegates, viewers, listeners, and friends. In recent weeks, our world has witnessed events that have reshaped how we see ourselves. Behind me are four members of a planet called Jevmmuns—originally settled by people from Earth thousands of years ago."

He paused, letting the weight of the moment settle.

141

"You've seen the destruction of the spacecraft that brought us back. I'm happy to report that we've recovered. I'm grateful to be here—and I'd like to share some thoughts."

Tobias's voice grew stronger.

"Here we are: the Humans of Earth. An evolving species on a quiet planet in a spiral galaxy. We orbit a star two-thirds out from the center of the Milky Way. From our vantage point, we see the galaxy as a white streak across the night sky—composed of stars like our sun."

He smiled. "We shouldn't brag, but we figured that out. That's impressive."

Laughter rippled through the room.

"But intelligence alone isn't enough. Do we understand ourselves? Each other? Do we have the wisdom to evolve—not just technologically, but emotionally and ethically?"

"We divide ourselves into nations, religions, races—false subdivisions that justify conflict. We forget our species and remember only our differences. We are, in many ways, a tragically flawed species."

"But I don't believe we're doomed. I believe we're afraid. And fear limits understanding. If we close our minds to what we know is right—love, kindness, forgiveness—we fall into hate, harshness, and intolerance."

"Our species cannot survive if we continue to disregard and destroy one another. Whether as individuals or as nations, we must move beyond our primal instincts."

Tobias looked out over the crowd.

"We fight over land, water, politics, ethnicity, religion—concepts rooted in the physical world or human invention. But there is hope."

He gestured to the Jevmmunians behind him.

"My friends have faced the same challenges. They've overcome division. They've preserved their environment, advanced medical care, and mastered space travel. They're not here to control us. They're here to show us—by example—that peace is possible."

Tobias turned to Beatrice. "On our last program, you began describing how your people overcame the same challenges we face on Earth. The transmission was cut short. Would you share more now?"

Beatrice rose gracefully and joined him at the podium.

"Thank you, Tobias," she said. "The key to peace and enlightenment is staying in touch with the observable natural universe. We rejected artificial concepts—race, nationality, and even money—when they conflicted with nature. We chose instead to serve the universe: growing crops, preserving the environment, helping others. Once we saw ourselves as one species, everything changed. We hope Earth will follow our example."

She returned to her seat. Tobias nodded, then continued.

"How do we reject the materialism and separateness ingrained in us? The Jevmmunians understand the threshold every sentient species must face: the divide between seeing ourselves as physical beings and recognizing ourselves as spiritual entities."

He paused, letting the weight of his words settle.

"The human dilemma is reconciling biology and spirit. Every challenge—war, intolerance, identity, environmental destruction—stems from this conflict. We believe we are our bodies, but we are not. We are our minds, emotions, energy—our spirit. The true person lives on long after the body is gone."

Tobias glanced at David, then at the Jevmmunians behind him. He felt a surge of inspiration, as if guided by something beyond himself.

"I am not unique. I am not special. We can all serve the divine energy of the universe. We fight over land, water, religion, politics—things we created, things that divide us. But we must shift our priorities. We must remember: humans are humans are humans."

He looked directly at the delegates.

"We must treat each other as individuals. We must use our intelligence to make decisions that benefit our species and our planet. We can all be a channel for the good. We are all in this together."

He paused, then said simply, "Thank you."

The General Assembly applauded—politely, but with a hunger for more. Tobias sensed they needed a blueprint, not just inspiration.

On the ride back to the hospital, Tobias sat between Beatrice and David in a long black limousine. He sighed, "We've got a lot more work to do."

For the next year, the group remained in protective custody. They could leave the hospital, but only with bodyguards. Tobias, David, Janice, Rebecca, Stokes, Beatrice, Goren, and Esmos all agreed to minimize public exposure. The attention was relentless. People clamored to see Tobias. Goren and Esmos drew constant curiosity. Beatrice and Stokes, as human Jevmmunians, became minor celebrities.

Tobias continued his weekly program from the hospital unit. He used it to educate the public about Earth's hidden history and its connection to Jevmmuns. He was careful not to portray Jevmmunian society as utopian. His goal was realism—avoiding self-destruction and building a better world.

Over the year, Tobias explored ancient mysteries: the Sphinx, pyramids in Africa and the Americas, Tiwanaku, Stonehenge, Easter Island, Puma Punku, the

Nazca lines. He explained their links to the Naku and the ancestors of the Jevmmunians. Each episode was eagerly anticipated, adding to Tobias's unwanted celebrity status.

He frequently interviewed Beatrice and Stokes. Goren appeared occasionally, when not working with Esmos and government officials. The two Naku were busy helping build a new spacecraft, funded by the UN and wealthy nations. Esmos agreed to assist only if the craft would serve both Earth and Jevmmuns.

The plan: return Goren, Esmos, Stokes, and Beatrice to Jevmmuns, accompanied by six UN delegates—one from each inhabited continent. Remarkably, the ship was completed within a year. Less than eighteen months after the crash on First Avenue, they were ready to announce the launch.

Over the course of the year, Tobias and Beatrice grew inseparable. Their bond deepened not only through frequent interviews on Tobias's program, but through long, quiet hours spent in each other's rooms, sharing stories of Jevmmuns and Earth. Their love had blossomed naturally—rooted in shared purpose and cosmic adventure.

One afternoon, as Tobias visited Beatrice to plan the next broadcast, she surprised him.

"You know, Tobias," she said, "you need someone from Jevmmuns to keep your story honest. I wouldn't want you misrepresenting my home planet."

Tobias feigned shock. "Me? I wouldn't dream of it."

They laughed, then kissed.

"Do you really think I need someone from Jevmmuns just to keep me honest?" he asked.

Beatrice smiled playfully. "Maybe I'll just make Earth my new home planet."

He replied, "Then maybe I'll make you my partner in life on Earth."

"Was that a proposal, Tobias?"

"I believe it was."

They embraced, knowing they'd been destined for each other all along.

Beatrice soon informed the Jevmmunians and the authorities of her decision to remain on Earth. Her first marriage to an Earthman would make her the second Mrs. Tobias Sinclair. Goren, Esmos, and Stokes understood and wished her well. No wedding date was set, but Tobias and Beatrice promised they'd be among the first invited—once they had a home of their own, on Earth or Jevmmuns.

By summer, the new spacecraft was ready. The launch would take place at the exact spot where the original ship had crash-landed—outside the UN building on First Avenue. This time, there were no secrets, no forest clearings, no Area 51. No threats. COL had not returned. The launch was a public celebration.

The media called it a milestone: from "The Great Landing" to "The Great Leaving." Crowds gathered along Manhattan's east side and the Queens riverfront. VIP seating lined First Avenue. Tobias, Beatrice, and David sat in the front row beside the UN Secretary General and other dignitaries.

As Goren, Stokes, Esmos, and the six UN delegates passed the reviewing stand, Tobias shook their hands.

Stokes handed Tobias a small device. "It transmits signals faster than light—through the wormhole. You'll hear from me in near real time."

"How is that possible?" Tobias asked.

"It's a one-way signal," Stokes said. "You can receive but not transmit."

"The story of my life," Tobias quipped. They laughed and embraced.

Stokes turned to David. "I hear beautiful sounds coming from your room. Music is the sound of our souls. Keep the guitar. Make more music."

"Thank you, sir… I mean, Stokes. I'll do my best."

Esmos, usually reserved, surprised them with a verbal farewell. "Goodbye. You make a lovely couple."

Tobias grinned. "So the cat didn't get your tongue after all!"

Esmos replied telepathically, "I still don't understand your riddles."

Beatrice smiled. "Don't worry, it wasn't that funny anyway."

Tobias bowed slightly. "Fly smoothly, navigator."

Esmos nodded telepathically, "Thank you."

Goren approached last, smiling warmly. "Perhaps you'll come to Jevmmuns next time."

Beatrice winked. "Maybe for our honeymoon."

Tobias added, "Or we'll split our time between both planets."

He grew solemn. "Goren, you've done more than anyone to introduce Jevmmuns to Earth. Your friend who inspired you—and your navigator who died in the crash—did not die in vain."

Goren nodded. "Their spirits are happy. We'll see each other again soon."

The crew boarded the ship. The ramp was retracted. The dome atop the saucer began to spin, casting a rainbow swirl of light into the late afternoon sky. The craft hovered above the UN building, then drifted over the East River. For a moment, it paused—symbolically bidding farewell to Earth.

Then, in a streak of white light, it vanished.

Tobias, Beatrice, Rebecca, Janice, and David had finally become a family. Though the public's fascination with Tobias and Beatrice waned slightly, they still required protection from lingering threats—especially from covert COL members still on Earth. Government officials determined that strict protective custody was no longer necessary. A more normal life could begin.

Tobias and Beatrice were married in a quiet civil ceremony, with plans for a larger celebration once life settled. The infamous Philadelphia house was sold, and the family relocated to a gated community on Long Island. It was peaceful, and close enough to Brooklyn for Tobias to continue working with Jimmy and Mill on the New School of Truth and his weekly broadcast.

Five months after the move, Tobias received a signal on the radio receiver Stokes had given him. Though months had passed on Earth, only days had passed aboard the ship traveling through the wormhole.

Stokes's voice crackled through the static.

"Tobias. Tobias. I hope you receive this message. You and Beatrice must listen! You must stay away from Jevmmuns. I repeat. You must stay away from Jevmmuns!"

Tobias called out to Beatrice. She entered the room as he turned up the volume.

"We arrived and orbited Jevmmuns—right into a civil war. They're fighting over *us*. Over whether to continue contact with Earth. The war began when the Council learned COL destroyed our ship. They thought we were dead. They retaliated. Now it's chaos."

148

"We tried to explain who we were, but they only saw our Earth-built ship. They thought we were spies. We couldn't land. Neither side trusts us. We're heading back to Earth. Hopefully, we'll be back in…"

A loud explosion interrupted the transmission. Static filled the room. The message looped, repeating itself endlessly.

Beatrice began to cry. Tobias held her as they stood motionless, absorbing the news. Her tears weren't of joy or sorrow—they were tears of pure, exhausted grief.

"They came here to save us," Tobias thought, "but they couldn't save Jevmmuns from itself."

Beatrice read his thoughts telepathically and sobbed harder.

"You're right, Tobias," she whispered. "Earth must follow its own path."

They kept the news to themselves. The UN remained silent. Two months passed with no further transmissions. The family settled into their new life. Rebecca watched shopping channels. Janice cooked and cared for her mother. David built a recording studio in the basement. Tobias and Beatrice adjusted to married life in their master suite. Government agents remained nearby, quietly vigilant.

Then, one month later, the radio crackled again. Stokes's voice returned—this time with Goren in the background.

"Tobias, Beatrice—we repaired the transmitter. The ship was damaged, but Earth-based materials held up better than expected. We're all okay."

Goren spoke clearly. "Greetings. We'll return to Earth tomorrow at 3 a.m. Please inform the UN. All six delegates are safe."

Stokes added with a chuckle, "Tobias, I hope you can get our cars back, man!"

Tobias rushed to tell Beatrice. She sat by the bedroom window, gazing at the sky.

"They're okay," he said. "They're coming back tomorrow."

Beatrice turned slowly, tears streaming down her cheeks. Not joy. Not sadness. Just relief.

Tobias contacted the UN and the authorities. First Avenue was cordoned off. No media announcements were made. Only a few passersby witnessed the landing.

Late at night, New York slowed to a sleepy rhythm. Limousines lined the street. Tobias and Beatrice sat in one. UN officials sat in another. Police cars and ambulances waited quietly.

At precisely 3 a.m., a streak of white light pierced the night sky. From its tip, the spacecraft emerged—seemingly out of thin air. Its multicolored dome lights joined the glow of city lamps, police cruisers, and ambulances, casting a kaleidoscopic shimmer across First Avenue.

The ship hovered briefly over the East River, then glided past the UN building and gently landed. Despite the late hour, crowds began to gather, held back by police barricades.

The ramp extended. Goren led the way, followed by the six UN delegates. Stokes and Esmos brought up the rear. They were greeted by the UN Secretary General, Tobias, Beatrice, and the Mayor of New York City. The group was whisked inside for a debriefing that lasted until dawn.

The spacecraft was returned to the government facility for analysis. Tobias and Beatrice were acknowledged as part of the team and invited to help plan future ventures into space.

Stokes, now too well-known to work undercover, joined the Sinclairs in their gated community. With his sister Greta still on Jevmmuns, Tobias and David became his closest family. He needed proximity—for safety and for healing.

Esmos remained in government facilities, working tirelessly with engineers to improve the spacecraft. Aloof but dedicated, he found purpose in navigation and construction.

Goren, however, posed a challenge. His fame made relocation impossible. He stayed at the hospital unit, studying medicine, astronomy, and spacecraft technology. Earth's limited resources frustrated him, but he remained committed.

Tobias visited Goren often. During one visit, he asked:

"Isn't it ironic? Earth is moving toward peace, while Jevmmuns—who came to help—is now at war. What does it mean?"

Goren replied telepathically:

"Both the pacifist and the warrior may taint one another."

Tobias nodded. "Neither side realized they were being changed by the other."

From that moment, Tobias and Goren became collaborators. Tobias's weekly program echoed Greta Stokes's mottos: This Behavior Is Beneath Us, We Are Better Than This, and his own: Remember: We Are All in This Together.

Public perception shifted. People began to see themselves as one species at a developmental crossroads. On his program, Tobias posed questions to provoke reflection:

"Can we use our intelligence without misusing it?"

"Are we too smart for our own good?"

"Will our discoveries destroy us—or save us?"

The evidence of alien contact, combined with Tobias's teachings, convinced many that the New Science offered a new way forward.

When the spacecraft was ready, the core team—Goren, Tobias, Beatrice, Stokes, and Esmos—reunited. Their first mission: return to Jevmmuns to mediate a cease-fire. The six UN delegates joined as observers and advisors.

"Those once in need of healing now serve as healers," Tobias said.

Goren added, "Humans must rise above the moment. From the bigger picture comes logic, objectivity, and peace."

This philosophy took root—on Earth and beyond. Earth was no longer seen as primitive, but as a planet capable of peace. Jevmmuns welcomed its cousins home.

Tobias's interstellar journeys were no longer solo missions. He brought David along, sharing the galaxy and its wonders. They visited other worlds, spreading peace through the example of Earth and Jevmmuns.

Tobias had tried to heal the world with the New Science. But in the end, he was most grateful for healing his family.

www.ingramcontent.com/pod-product-compliance
Lightning Source LLC
Chambersburg PA
CBHW020404030726
47496CB00007B/2301